TEMPTING ALIBI

Savannah Stuart

Cover art: Jaycee of Sweet 'N Spicy Designs
Author website: www.savannahstuartauthor.com

Tempting Alibi/Katie Reus. – 2nd ed.

ISBN-13: 9781502520548
ISBN-10: 1502520540

eBook ISBN: 9780996087476

To my wonderful sister.

Praise for the books of Savannah Stuart

"Fans of sexy paranormal romance should definitely treat themselves to this sexy & fun story." —Nina's Literary Escape

"I enjoyed this installment so much I'll be picking up book one...worth the price for the punch of plot and heat." —Jessie, HEA USA Today blog

"...a scorching hot read." —The Jeep Diva

"This story was a fantastic summer read!" —Book Lovin' Mamas

"If you're looking for a hot, sweet read, be sure not to miss Tempting Alibi. It's one I know I'll revisit again and again." —Happily Ever After Reviews

"You will not regret reading the previous story or this one. I would recommend it to anyone who loves a great shifter story." —The Long & Short of It (Power Unleashed)

"...a fun and sexy shapeshifter book and definitely worth the read." —The Book Binge

Scott O'Callaghan pulled off his T-shirt as he reached the end of his six mile run. It didn't matter that he'd been out of the Marine Corps for years, running had been ingrained into him long ago. At least he wasn't carrying a twenty pound rucksack. Leaves crunched under his sneakers as he headed up the path from the lake to his house.

He'd moved into his place a few months ago and liked living outside of town. He'd opened *O'Callaghan's Auto Body Shop* about five years ago. In the beginning he'd practically lived there but what he really wanted was to live close, but not so much that he didn't have an escape from work. Now that business was steady and he was turning a profit he'd decided to move to Hudson Lake where it was quieter. Not that his small hometown was exactly bustling, but he preferred the relative peace the lake offered.

The only problem was his neighbor. Okay, she wasn't actually a problem. She was just a big damn distraction. On instinct he glanced in the direction of her house.

He rubbed his T-shirt over his damp face and nearly froze when he saw *her.*

Michaela Miller.

In a bikini. On her back porch.

Just like that his body reacted. The woman was toned and sleek with the perfect amount of curves. She owned a yoga studio in town so it made sense that she was in shape. But *damn.* Her back was to him and she was wearing those Brazilian-style bottoms showing off her tight ass. He shifted uncomfortably and tried to order his feet to move.

Normally he ran early in the morning and never saw her before heading to work. But it was Sunday and since he was off he'd gotten a late start. He'd seen her coming up from the lake sometimes after a swim, but she'd always had a T-shirt and shorts on, or a towel wrapped around her. He'd never seen her like this.

Now his fantasies, which were already out of control, were just going to get worse. It didn't matter that fantasizing about the sexy redhead was beyond stupid. Michaela Miller was so far out of his league it wasn't even a little funny. He'd grown up in a trailer park on the outskirts of town and she'd grown up in a fucking mansion. One of those historical homes right smack-dab in the middle of downtown.

As if she sensed his presence, she looked over her shoulder. When she saw him she smiled and waved.

And he just stared. Like an idiot.

He should say something. Wave back. He started to but she'd already turned away.

Fuck.

Shaking his head at himself, he hurried into his house and let the door slam shut behind him. He needed a cold shower. A long one.

A few hours later he pushed open the door to one of the only local sports bars in Hudson Creek. Daniel and some of the other guys from work had asked him to come up and have a few beers.

Since he was their boss he tended not to go out with them too often. When he had the power to fire them it just felt wrong. Daniel was the only exception. With the man's work ethic Scott couldn't imagine ever letting him go. Two steps inside and he spotted Daniel at the bar talking to a woman.

There weren't any important games on the televisions, but for a regular afternoon the place was packed. Probably because it was balls hot outside and people were either out boating and jet skiing, at the local sports bars, or at barbeques. Summers in small towns were like that.

As Scott moved through some of the high-top tables to the bar, Daniel spotted him and nodded in his direction. The woman with him turned around and Scott realized it was his friend's sister.

One of them. Darby or Devon. He couldn't tell the twins apart to save his life. At least not until they spoke. Darby was softer spoken and Devon was loud and boisterous. But on the outside the two blonds looked exactly the same. Like pinup models from the fifties. Something Scott heard more often than not from guys ragging on Daniel about his sisters at the shop.

"Hey man, we were just talking about getting a table," Daniel said, swiveling on his bar stool. "The guys aren't here yet."

Scott didn't care where they sat. He just wanted a cold beer and to try to get his sexy neighbor off his mind. Because that shower hadn't helped any.

"I hope you don't mind me joining you two until my friends show up," his sister said, her tone soft. Darby then.

Scott shook his head. "Course not. D, what are you drinking?" he asked, waving down the bartender.

While they grabbed one of the only open tables Scott bought a round. As he approached the table, Daniel was talking quietly into his phone, his jaw clenched tight.

"He'll probably be a few minutes. Cray-cray time." Darby rolled her eyes and took the Corona he slid to her with a 'thanks'.

Scott snorted. "Which one is it now?" Because Daniel dated more women in a month than Scott had in the past couple years. And the man was always arguing with them. They wanted a commitment and he didn't. He'd finally taken to turning off his phone during the work day.

Darby's lips pursed together as she shook her head. "I don't even ask their names anymore. So," she said, changing the subject, "My friend Michaela tells me you're her new-ish neighbor."

He blinked as Darby's words settled in. Michaela had talked about him? "Uh, yeah." He'd moved there a few months ago so they were fairly new neighbors.

"You like living out on the lake?"

He nodded, trying to find his voice. He didn't have a problem talking with women. Ever. Until Michaela. Even hearing her name got him twisted up. Which was stupid as fuck. "Yep."

Darby snickered. "Man, she said you were quiet."

He blinked again. "Yeah?"

"Yep." Her lips twitched before she took a sip of her beer. "She should be up here pretty soon."

Just like that his heart started beating triple time. He opened his mouth to respond when his phone buzzed in his pocket. Glancing at the caller ID he frowned. It was a local area code but he didn't know the number. Still, sometimes he got emergency calls over the weekend.

Living in a small town had its advantages and disadvantages. His shop was closed Sundays but if someone needed help immediately he wasn't going to say no. And everyone knew it.

He murmured an apology to Darby and answered his phone. "Hello?"

"Scott?" It was his dad. The drunk bastard who only called when he was out of cash or booze.

Sighing, Scott motioned to Darby that he was going to step outside. Unfortunately he had a feeling he wouldn't be staying long after this call. Resentment surged through him that his old man chose now of all times to call. Part of him hated that he wouldn't get to stick around and actually talk to Michaela, but the other part of him was relieved he couldn't say anything stupid and completely ruin his chance with her.

Not that he actually thought he had one.

CHAPTER TWO

Three months later

Michaela froze with her glass of wine halfway to her mouth. Her eyes widened as she watched her sexy-as-sin neighbor, Scott, step through his back door and strip out of his T-shirt. He glanced around, once in her direction, then toward the house on the other side of his own before stripping his pants off.

Underneath he wore shorts that should be illegal. She knew he'd been in the Marine Corps before settling back in Hudson Creek and those were his—silkies or softies—or some other ridiculous name. Whatever the damn things were called, they barely covered his crotch and they put all sorts of bad thoughts in her mind. The man obviously wore them to drive her insane. Every morning he was up at dawn and jogging around the lake they lived on and showing off all sorts of taut, lean muscles and tattoos. And she'd only discovered that by accident. She'd gotten up early one morning months ago and had seen him run by her place at the ungodly hour. Now mornings were her favorite time of the day.

She felt a bit like a pervert but it was hard to care. Seemed she was getting a double show today though. Apparently his morning workout wasn't enough and he was getting in some extra time tonight. And he clearly had no clue she was watching. The light bulb on her back porch had blown a week ago and she'd been too lazy to replace it. Usually the moonlight and stars reflecting off the lake gave her enough light anyway, but the sky was overcast tonight and she was sitting in relative darkness.

Her hand tightened around her glass as he reached up and grabbed on to the metal bar he'd installed recently. It was attached to some sort of pole thing and now she realized why he'd mounted it. Michaela's stomach fluttered as he started doing pull-ups. If she had popcorn, tonight would be perfect.

Up and down, up and down. Those big arms clenched and tightened each time he pulled up. It was beyond embarrassing, but her panties dampened as she watched him move. For such a bulky guy, he moved with a fluid grace that made her wonder what he'd be like beneath the sheets.

He was male perfection. Dark hair, dark piercing eyes and not an inch of fat on that hard body. Unfortunately he was quiet as hell and no doubt thought she was an idiot. Scott was from the area, but he'd been gone for years. He'd opened his auto body shop five years ago but she'd never really talked to him. She'd been away at college when he first moved back anyway.

But he'd moved to the lake seven months ago so she'd brought him cookies to welcome him to the neighborhood. Everyone who lived on Hudson Lake knew everyone and she'd wanted to do something nice. When she'd shown up with her plate, he'd grunted something incomprehensible, then just stared at her as she rambled on for a full two minutes about—God, what was it? She couldn't even remember now but since he'd barely responded to her neighborly gesture, she'd steered clear of the sexy man. Didn't mean she couldn't admire what was placed in front of her.

After the pull-ups, he started on the sit-ups. When he switched to push-ups, she shook her head and slipped through her back door. Nearly an hour had passed and if she wasn't careful, she'd combust from watching him.

She had to get up early to teach a yoga class anyway. Thursdays were her early days and her patrons paid good money for her to do her job right. She wasn't going to come in late and tired because she'd been horny and spying on her neighbor.

* * *

"Hey, boss, would you sign off on this?"

Scott glanced up from filling out the payroll as Daniel walked into his office holding a clipboard. "What is it?"

"I just finished with Mr. Wilkinson's BMW. I'm gonna call and let him know if that's all right."

"Sounds good." Scott quickly scribbled his signature without reading the paperwork. Daniel had been with him since he'd opened *O'Callaghan's Auto Body Shop* five years ago. He was the most trustworthy employee he had. And Scott hated micromanaging. If he had to be on someone's ass 24/7 to check up on them, he didn't need them as an employee.

Daniel cleared his throat. "Thanks. By the way, I just saw Michaela Miller drive up. Thought you'd like to take that one personally."

That got Scott's attention. "Get the hell out of here," he muttered.

Chuckling to himself, Daniel quickly left the office.

Scott wiped his dirty palms on his work pants. His mouth filled with cotton at the mere mention of *her* name. Anytime the sexy woman got near him, he lost the ability to think, let alone speak. He'd lived through boot camp, SERE school, and about a dozen other brutal training programs during his eight years in the Marine Corps. Not to mention he'd lived in a warzone for six of those years. But for some reason he couldn't talk to his petite, redheaded neighbor for longer than a couple minutes without breaking into a nervous sweat. It was fucking embarrassing.

The sound of the bell jingling on the front door pushed him into action. He turned off his computer screen and exited his office.

Michaela stood behind the counter with her car keys in hand. She smiled when she saw him. "Hi, I think my car needs to see a doctor."

His gut clenched as her face lit up. *Talk,* he ordered his mouth. "What's the problem?"

She shrugged and her smile faded a fraction. "I have no idea. On my way to work this morning, it started making these little chugging sounds. Like it was coughing or something. I figured maybe I could leave it with you and stop back by when I'm done with work... Of course that's only if you can fit me in. I know you're busy and—"

"I'll fit you in." He wished he could smile or do something to put her more at ease but all he could think about was pushing down those tight black yoga pants she wore and sliding his cock into her tight body. He didn't know how, but he knew she'd be tight. As far as he was aware, his neighbor didn't date. Or she hadn't since he'd moved in. Not that he'd been paying attention. *Much.*

"Okay, well I guess I'll just leave my keys here. Do you want me to fill out some paperwork or anything?"

"Yeah." Good for him. Another word. Reaching under the counter, he started to pass her the information form when he spotted Sheriff Hill slamming his car door shut. He cursed under his breath.

"What?" Michaela asked, confusion evident in her pale gray eyes.

"Wh...oh, nothing." He realized she thought he'd been talking to her. As the front door opened, Scott braced himself for more bullshit from the sheriff. The man had never liked him but lately it seemed as if he'd kicked his harassment up a notch. And Scott couldn't figure out why.

Michaela turned at the sound of the bell. "Hi, Sheriff," she murmured before returning to her paperwork.

"Morning, Michaela." Just as quick, the older man turned his hard stare on Scott. His dark eyes narrowed. "Hello, Mr. O'Callaghan. Was wondering if you'd be able to provide an alibi for where you were last night."

And there it was. No preamble. No niceties. Nothing. The son of a bitch had been in here hassling him for the past couple of months for no reason. Scott gritted his teeth. He hated that this was happening in front of Michaela of all people. Or hell, any customer. This was bullshit and bordering on harassment and he wasn't going to put up with it. He knew his fucking rights. "Who wants to know?"

The sheriff stepped closer, his expression darkening. "I do. How about you show me some respect, son? There was a robbery down at my nephew's shop last night. Got the guy on video."

Out of the corner of his eye, Scott could see Michaela watching them and he wanted to knock the sheriff's teeth in. "First of all, I'm not your son. And second, if you've got the guy on video, why are you here hassling me about it?"

"He was wearing a mask but he's got your build." The sheriff leaned forward a fraction in what Scott supposed was meant to be an intimidating manner but after having a tough bastard as his drill sergeant, the sheriff was like the Easter bunny.

"What time was this, Sheriff?" Michaela asked.

In surprise, they both turned toward her.

"About eight," Sheriff Hill grunted.

"Well rest easy then, sir, because Scott was with me."

Scott's mouth dropped open but he snapped it shut before the sheriff swiveled back toward him.

The old man's eyes narrowed. "Is that right?"

Before he could answer, Michaela interrupted. "That *is* right. I'll head down to the station right now and make an official statement if you'd like. I'll even call my brother and have him meet me there in case I need *legal* representation." Her voice was unexpectedly haughty. "In fact, it sounds like Scott might need representation if you have official questions for him. Maybe we should just all head down there now and I'll call Jake." Her voice was sugar sweet, but there was a surprising edge to it. One the sheriff would have to be stupid to miss.

The sheriff didn't even glance at her. "That won't be necessary. You haven't seen the last of me," he muttered to Scott before stalking from the building.

Scott turned his gaze on Michaela, wondering what the hell she was doing. She pushed the paperwork and her keys toward him. "I get off work at four. I'll be back to pick up my car then."

Before he could string two words together, she'd turned on her heel and was out the door. The last glimpse he got was of that tight backside of hers strutting across the street. Her yoga studio was the next block over and it wasn't too cold so he knew she wouldn't have a problem walking. Still, he wished he'd have offered to drive her or something.

Why the hell had she told the sheriff he'd been with her last night? He wasn't guilty of anything, but she didn't know that. Scott was from the wrong side of the tracks and she was most definitely from the right side. Her family was well-known and respected throughout the county so he knew she wasn't giving him an alibi simply so he'd fix her car for free. Just what was she up to?

CHAPTER THREE

Sheriff Terrance Hill steered down the street in his Crown Vic, his jaw clenched tightly. That Scott O'Callaghan was just as useless as his father. Just because he'd been in the Marines didn't mean he was a damn war hero.

Too bad that's what most people in town seemed to think. He looked like a thug with all those tattoos. Some people were just no good. And Terrance's nephew swore O'Callaghan was out to get him.

Frank had never been a liar either. He wasn't as good at business as his father, Terrance's brother, had been, but his auto body shop had been doing well enough.

Until Scott blazed back into town and opened his.

For a while though, they'd seemed to have pretty equal business. Hudson Creek wasn't huge, but a little competition was a good thing. Kept prices fair. Terrance could appreciate that.

But Frank was convinced that O'Callaghan had broken into his place and was sabotaging him.

A few minutes later he pulled into the *Hill Family Auto Body Shop* parking lot. Place had been here for two generations. He didn't like the thought of his nephew having to go under.

When he stepped into the lobby, the little bell above the glass door jingled overhead. Frowning, he looked around. No one was behind the main desk. Normally Lyla, Frank's wife was running things.

She hadn't been around lately though. Terrance frowned, stepping around the desk. He opened the door into the garage. Faint music played from somewhere. Looking around, he started to worry until he saw Frank's legs sticking out from under an older model sedan.

"Frank," he called out, making his way around one of the pits until he reached the middle one.

When his nephew didn't respond, Terrance nudged him in the calf.

Frank jerked and rolled out from under the car, his eyes red-rimmed and bleary.

"Were you sleeping under there?" Terrance demanded.

Rubbing at his eyes and streaking grease over his cheek, Frank shook his head and pushed up from the rolling board. "Nah, just dozing for a second. Had a rough night," he muttered as he stood.

"Where's Lyla?" Terrance wondered if they'd been fighting and Frank had gone off drinking. He sure looked like hell. But it surprised him Lyla wasn't here, she was so dependable.

Frank shrugged and avoided eye contact, a sure sign he didn't want to talk about it. Well too bad.

"You two having problems?"

"Nothing I can't handle. We're fine, we . . . it's just stupid married stuff, that's all."

Terrance nodded, deciding to leave it alone for now. Lyla was a good woman, had been a good influence on Frank since they got married. He loved his nephew but he wasn't blind to his faults. He was a good enough husband but he could certainly take care of Lyla better. Women liked to know they were appreciated. "I talked to O'Callaghan and he's not the guy who broke into your place." He wished his nephew had actually fixed his security equipment because unlike what he'd told O'Callaghan, Terrance didn't have actual video proof. He'd just been hoping Scott would slip up.

Frank snorted and turned away from him, stalking to where the radio was on a far wall. He turned it off. "And you just believed him?"

"No, he's got an alibi." A very credible one. Terrance wasn't sure if Michaela Miller was actually dating that thug or if they were just friends. He knew O'Callaghan had moved out by the lake though, so they could just be neighbors.

His nephew snorted again and shoved his hands in the pockets of his dark blue coveralls. "I don't believe it. He's out to get me. Has been from the moment he opened that shop of his."

Terrance didn't respond, not wanting to get him riled up. Glancing around the shop, his frown deepened. It wasn't lunchtime and it was late enough that everyone should be here. "Where's your staff?"

"Didn't have much work today so I told the guys not to come in."

That sure as hell wasn't going to help Frank's business. If the guys weren't working, they'd start looking elsewhere to make money. "It wouldn't hurt to open up your garage doors and clean up the lobby." The place wasn't filthy and yes, people had certain expectations since it was an auto body shop, but still, dusting and straightening it wouldn't hurt. Not to mention keeping the shop's phone near him. How the hell was Frank supposed to take customer calls all the way over here with no one answering the phones?

"Now you sound like Lyla," he muttered, grabbing a tool and bending back down to the rolling board. He avoided eye contact as he did.

Damn it. Terrance rubbed a hand over his face as his nephew rolled back under the car and out of sight. After his brother had died a decade ago he'd taken to looking after Frank, but the boy just wasn't motivated. Not like his daddy had been. He didn't want to make him feel like he had to live up to anything, but showing some pride in the business you owned should be something Frank did on his own.

"Why don't you and Lyla come over for dinner tonight?"

"I'll let you know later, but I don't think we're gonna make it. She's got a Zumba class or something tonight."

"All right, see ya later." As he left, Terrance thought about calling Lyla to see what was really going on with Frank, but decided not to. He could try to help his nephew out but he couldn't poke his nose where it didn't belong. And marriage stuff was private. Terrance had been married for thirty years and loved his wife. They rarely argued but if they did, they didn't talk to others about it.

He looked at his nephew's building as he reached his car and leaned against the front door. The place could definitely use a new coat of paint. The name of the business was faded, the rolling doors were down and even though the open sign was turned on, the place still looked as if it was closed.

Didn't help that there weren't any vehicles other than his own out in front of the shop. Part of him wondered if there had been a break-in at all, but Frank had filed a police report and Terrance had seen the damage himself. It was hard to imagine his nephew going to all that trouble to file a fake report. And he couldn't imagine what other motive he could have when Terrance knew his insurance policy wasn't that high—and his deductible would cost him too much to make it worth it to file a claim with them. So monetary gain was out.

Someone had to have broken into his place. It could have been petty thieves, but nothing had been taken. Frank said his computer had been messed with though.

Getting into his Crown Vic, Terrance started the engine. Whatever was going on, he needed to keep an eye on that O'Callaghan bastard. Once a screw up, always a screw up, as far as he was concerned. Especially since the man's father was worthless.

And Terrance doubted the apple fell far from the tree.

CHAPTER FOUR

Michaela frowned when she heard her doorbell ring. Her brothers weren't supposed to stop by until Saturday and she wasn't expecting anyone else. It was after dark and her family knew to call first. Of course they didn't always listen. She might be living on her own, but her family liked to keep tabs on her, especially her brothers. Not that she actually minded.

Her feet were silent along the wooden hallway until she reached the front door. When she peered through the peephole, her heart skipped a beat.

It was Scott.

All six feet of him. He hadn't been at the shop earlier when she'd picked up her car. One of his guys had given her little Volkswagen Beetle a clean bill of health—free of charge. Which had been incredibly nice and unexpected. But Scott had been nowhere to be seen. The disappointment she'd experienced had been surprisingly acute.

Glancing down at herself, she cringed. She wore a pair of old, faded jeans, a plain white T-shirt and no bra. She thought about racing upstairs to put one on but was afraid he'd be gone by the time she got back. The man was so quiet and elusive she wasn't passing up this chance to actually talk to him in a relaxed setting.

Taking a calming breath, she opened the door. Her eyes widened when she realized he had a small bouquet of daffodils and a bottle of wine. She couldn't remember the last time a man had given her flowers. Except her brothers on her birthday, but that didn't count. "Hey, neighbor." She was glad her voice sounded normal.

"Hi." Scott smiled—sort of—for the first time since she'd met him, and a tiny dimple appeared in his left cheek. The action softened his sharp features and made her stomach do annoying little flip-flops.

It appeared he wasn't going to speak so she broke the silence. "Are those for me?"

"Oh right. Yeah." He practically shoved them at her but didn't make a move to step inside.

Okay, so apparently he needed some help. Normally she liked a man to take charge, but good Lord, she wanted Scott O'Callaghan in a bad way so she'd make an exception. He'd been staring in way too many of her fantasies recently. "I'm going to put these in some water. Would you like to come in?"

He raked a hand through his dark hair and nodded. "Yeah."

Without waiting for him, she turned and headed back down the hallway toward her kitchen. She heard the door shut behind him, then his heavy boots thud along the floor. As she pulled out a vase from one of the cabinets, she glanced over her shoulder to find him checking out her ass. Grinning to herself, she quickly averted her gaze then filled up the vase with water. At least she knew he was interested. Over the summer she thought she'd seen him checking her out a couple times when she'd been out swimming, but he was so hard to read she hadn't been sure.

She placed the flowers in the middle of her round kitchen table and motioned for him to sit. "Do you want something to drink?"

He shook his head but sat. And he still held on to that bottle of wine. She assumed it was for her but wasn't going to ask.

"So, why are you here?" Might as well get right to the point.

His dark eyes narrowed on her face for a moment. Then that unreadable mask slid back in place. "Why'd you lie to the sheriff today?"

Michaela tried to ignore the heat she could feel creeping into her cheeks. She didn't want to sound like some sort of stalker but she needed to come clean. "I saw you last night working out on your porch and you were outside for over an hour around the time he mentioned. Besides, I knew you wouldn't steal anything."

His dark eyebrows snapped down in confusion. "How can you know that?"

She shrugged. "I just do. You don't rip off any of your customers and I know the sheriff's nephew is losing money at his auto shop because of you."

It was nearly imperceptible, but his eyes flared with disbelief.

She decided to answer his unspoken question. "It's a small town and people talk. They'd rather come to you than to that lazy bastard, Frank Hill. My guess is he sent his uncle, the *good* sheriff, to mess with you. He probably gave him a sob story or some crap." Michaela wasn't certain the sheriff was actually crooked, but he was too antiquated in his thinking. He thought way too much like a 'good ol' boy'. Elections were coming up and her oldest brother was working on a campaign to get one of their uncles elected. For the past few elections there simply hadn't been any options other than Sheriff Hill, but her family and a few others knew it was time for a change.

Scott hadn't even thought about that. As a teenager, before he'd joined the Marines, he'd gotten in to his fair share of trouble boosting cars. Nothing he ever did any time for, but he just figured that's why the sheriff had been giving him so much grief lately. Old grudges or some other bullshit. On more than one occasion the man had made it clear he thought Scott was just a thug and that he was waiting for him to screw up. This revelation actually made more sense.

As he stared into Michaela's pale eyes, he managed to get it together. In all his thirty-one years he'd never had a problem talking to women. As a rule he didn't talk much anyway, but he'd never been nervous.

Until her.

He unclenched his hand from the bottle and slid it across the table to her. "Thank you...for what you did. You saved me a big headache. I've seen you drinking wine on your back porch sometimes. Wasn't sure what you liked, but the lady at Tessa's Wine Mart said it was good and that you'd like it." He shrugged as he trailed off. Hot damn, he managed three full sentences. That must be some sort of record.

She looked just as surprised as he felt. Her soft lips curved up into a pretty smile and her cheeks stained an even darker shade of pink. "Thanks. You want a glass— or I've got beer if you'd prefer."

"Beer's fine." He stood and pushed his chair back. "Where's your bottle opener? I'll pour you a glass."

She pointed to the drawer next to her sink as she opened her refrigerator. As he retrieved the opener, he glanced around her kitchen. Natural wood flooring, darker wood cabinets—with a built in wine rack—copper pots hanging from a pot rack over the center island and terracotta utensil holders. He didn't know shit about styles but he thought it was called French country or something. Whatever it was, it fit her. Classic and beautiful.

"I'll meet you on the back porch," she said as she opened the back door and disappeared from sight.

Once he'd poured her a glass, he found her sitting on the cushioned porch swing facing the lake. He placed her drink next to his beer on the glass table in front of them before sitting beside her. The swing creaked slightly, but it was sturdy. When he glanced at her, he found her staring at him with a curious expression on her face.

For the first time in over a decade he felt like a randy teenager with a crush. What the hell was he supposed to talk to her about? His chance was finally here and he didn't want to screw it up. He cleared his throat. "Temperature's supposed to drop about twenty degrees tonight."

Now her lips curved up even more. "Are we really going to talk about the weather?" The question was said softly and with a slight trace of humor. But there was no mistaking the desire in her eyes.

His abs clenched as her pale eyes flared a shade darker. With the moon and stars above, they had the perfect amount of illumination. Everything about the moment was perfect. He didn't want to ruin it by opening his mouth. Probably because he always said the wrong thing. When he was a kid, talking usually got him a beating from his old man. So, he'd learned to keep his mouth shut. Then in the Corps, he'd been a sniper, which meant missions by himself for months at a time. What the hell did he need words for anyway? The way Michaela was looking at him now made him realize she didn't want to talk either.

That was good. Very good. He might not be good with words, but he was good with his mouth.

Leaning forward, he reached out and cupped her jaw. His grip was gentle. If she wanted to pull away, he wouldn't stop her. But she didn't. Instead, those perfect lips of hers parted invitingly and her breathing became uneven.

His cock pressed painfully against his zipper as his gaze zeroed in on that full mouth. When her pink tongue darted out and moistened her lips, he had to bite back a groan. He could only imagine what it would feel like to have her tongue lick and kiss his shaft.

He'd spent the past seven months acting like a coward and he wasn't going to pass up this opportunity. It was as if someone had given him the keys to the city. Closing the distance between them, he covered her mouth with his.

She tasted like strawberries. Sweet and sensual. Maybe she'd been eating fruit before he came by. As his tongue rasped against hers, his cock jutted forward as if it had a mind of its own. Oh yeah, his body knew this was the chance of a lifetime and he wasn't passing this up. He didn't care if it was pathetic, whatever she gave, he was taking.

He threaded his fingers through her hair and moved a few inches closer, not wanting to move too fast. When he did, she moaned a throaty sound that went straight to all his nerve endings. It was too soon, but before he could change his mind, he dropped his hand cupping her head and grasped her hips. Damn, he hoped this wasn't too fast for her.

Still kissing her, he pulled her over his lap so that she straddled him. The need to feel her on him like this was overwhelming. She let out a surprised cry when his hips rolled against hers.

She pulled her head back a fraction and simply stared at him, her eyes burning with hunger. For once, it seemed the redhead was speechless.

Her hard nipples were visible through her t-shirt. Teasing him. Taunting him. Clearly she'd temporarily lost her mind and he wasn't going to pass up the opportunity to see her breasts. On more than one occasion he'd jerked off to the fantasy of Michaela stretched out under him. On top of him. Up against the wall. On her back porch. It didn't matter. In all those fantasies he'd wondered about her nipples. The size, the shape, the color.

It was likely too soon to make another move, but he didn't want to stop touching her. He grasped the hem of her shirt and slowly started to push it up. When she lifted her arms above her head he didn't waste time. He finished tugging it off and his breath caught in his throat as he drank in the sight of her.

Her teardrop shaped breasts were absolute perfection. Slightly bigger than he'd realized. And her nipples were a unique rose color. A little darker than pink, but not quite red. Like little candies for him to suck on. They peaked even harder under his gaze. When she went to cover herself, he circled both her wrists with his hands and held them at her side. Not hard, but enough so that she couldn't move.

Meeting her gaze, he could see uncertainty on her face and that surprised the hell out of him. He didn't know how to tell her she had nothing to be insecure about so he leaned forward and stroked his tongue over one of the hardened buds. As she trembled under his kisses, he let her hands go.

Michaela couldn't believe she was sitting on her back porch, half-naked with walking, sometimes-talking, sex Scott O'Callaghan. It was all too surreal and wonderful. He might be shy around her but he sure wasn't acting that way right now. For that she was thankful. She didn't want to have to teach anyone what to do between the sheets. She wasn't even sure it'd get that far, at least not tonight, but something told her that the two of them eventually getting naked together was inevitable. Like the sun rising every morning.

When he raked his teeth over one of her nipples, she clutched on to his hard shoulders and grinded her hips against him. An unbearable heat burned low in her belly. Her panties were completely damp and all he'd done was kiss her breasts.

If he was this good with his mouth, no wonder he rarely talked. The man didn't need to. Of course, she didn't like the thought of him doing this with anyone but her. She quickly brushed that thought aside and focused on the here and now. On what he was going with his talented, wicked tongue.

His tongue swiped around her areola, then he kissed a moist path on the underside and the sides of her breast. He wasn't leaving anything untouched. Almost as if he were branding her, making sure he covered every single inch of her.

The thought sent a shiver rolling over her. As he teased her with his tongue, he palmed her other breast.

Through heavy-lidded eyes, she watched as he strummed her nipple. He had a tattoo of some sort of snake that curled around his forearm all the way down to his wrist. Watching it move as he continued his heavenly assault turned her on even more. She wanted to kiss and lick it, to feel him tense and flex under her.

From his mouth and fingers alone she was so close to coming. Something she hadn't thought possible. "Scott." She whispered his name, mainly because she wanted to hear it. But mostly because she desperately needed to say it. *Scott.* They were not going to go back to acting like simple neighbors after this where he barely said two words to her in a whole month. She couldn't bear it.

When she said his name again, his entire body jerked against her. His hips pushed up and her throat clenched when his erection rubbed against her lower abdomen. The man was huge, something she should have guessed given his size. Not tonight—she wasn't ready—but she knew that soon enough, she was going to see his hard length and her entire body tensed in anticipation at the thought.

He leaned closer and brushed his lips against the sensitive spot behind her ear. "I want to touch you here, Michaela." As if she didn't understand what he meant, he placed his large hand over her denim-covered mound.

"Okay," she whispered.

Lightning fast, as if he was afraid she'd change her mind, he unbuttoned her jeans and pulled the zipper down. The sound cut through the quiet of the cool night. He didn't try to take them off the rest of the way and he didn't make a move toward his own clothes. Which made her feel secure. He was doing this for her without any pressure for more. That just made her want him even more.

He slid his hand under the flimsy lace material of her panties and cupped her mound. For a moment she was almost embarrassed by how wet she was but when he groaned and raked his teeth against her neck, she let go of her insecurities. She was slick, completely soaked, and all because of him. All for him. When he rubbed his middle finger over her swollen clit, she let go of her control.

It was like he'd released some switch inside of her. She'd been ready to come with the stimulation of her nipples alone. Combined with how much Scott's mere presence seemed to get her riled up, and this added pleasure was too much. It seemed impossible to believe that she could get off so easily, but when he started rubbing against her clit in a steady rhythm, she pushed up on her knees and held his shoulders in a death grip. Her thighs strained as she tried to squeeze her legs together.

Nothing could ease her ache now though, nothing but Scott. He switched breasts and sucked her other nipple between his teeth with an intense tug. The action pushed her right over the edge. Her climax curled through her like a slow building wave until it crested and crashed throughout her entire body. It slammed into all her nerve endings, making her shudder as wave after wave of pleasure punched through her.

It seemed to go on forever. She held onto him, not caring that she was moaning his name and other dirty things.

Even as her orgasm subsided, he continued rubbing his finger over her clit. The tiny bundle of nerves was raw and ultra-sensitized. Mercifully he finally withdrew his hand.

Her fingers and toes tingled with the aftereffects. This had been the last thing she'd expected tonight. Now that she had Scott where she wanted him, she didn't want to let him go.

His gaze was on hers, burning hot as he watched her, as if he wanted to memorize every inch of her face. When he lifted his hand to his mouth and tasted his fingers—*tasted her*—she thought she might come again. That was the single hottest thing she'd ever witnessed a man do.

"Don't leave." The words were out before she could stop herself. The last thing she wanted was to sound like some needy freak, but she wanted him to spend the night with her. She rushed on. "I don't mean to have sex. I just want you to stay—"

"Okay." His charcoal eyes seemed even darker under the moonlight. The answer was so simple. He didn't need her explanations or anything. He just said okay. The quickness of his response stunned her so much she couldn't think of a response.

Before she realized what he was doing, he hooked his hands around her backside and stood, pulling her with him. He snagged her discarded T-shirt as he strode toward the back door so she wrapped her arms tighter around his neck and let him carry her inside. His heart beat wildly against his chest and she could feel it almost as if it were her own. She couldn't explain it, even to herself, but she'd never felt so connected to another person. For the first time in her life, she realized talking was overrated.

CHAPTER FIVE

Thwap! Thwap!

Michaela opened her eyes and glared at the digital clock on her nightstand. It was barely daylight. *What was all that racket?* Groaning, she rolled over and saw that Scott's side of the bed was empty.

Immediately, the air rushed from her lungs. Had he left in the middle of the night? No. She quickly discarded that thought. He wasn't a jerk. That much she knew. They'd spent the rest of the night cuddling and kissing and simply wrapped up in each other's arms. It had been incredibly sweet and unexpected. She'd tried to take things a little further, but he'd been incredibly dominating and seemed intent on taking his time. The little take-charge streak had surprised her. Well, surprised and pleased.

Thwap! It was coming from outside.

Muttering curses to herself, she pushed her thick comforter off and got out of bed. As soon as her bare feet hit the wood floor, a chill snaked down her spine. Scott was right. The temperature had definitely dropped and she needed to turn her heat on. Since she was only wearing panties, she also needed warmer clothes. After tugging on a pair of thick fleece pants and a matching sweater, she headed downstairs.

As she checked the paltry pile of wood next to her fireplace, she spotted Scott through one of her living room windows chopping wood. A curious warmth curled through her. That's what the sound was. Suddenly her annoying wakeup call wasn't so annoying after all.

Smiling to herself, she made her way to the kitchen and started a pot of coffee. Once the smell of rich French roast permeated the air, she slipped on her boots and walked out the back door and around the house.

Scott glanced up mid-swing and gave her that adorable half-smile she was coming to crave before he sliced another piece of wood in two. Which was incredibly hot; both the wood chopping and the smile. Now that he was comfortable around her, he didn't seem to be so nervous. And those smiles were absolutely disarming. Even more so because she knew he wasn't trying to get her turned on when he did.

This morning he wore a long-sleeved flannel shirt and jeans, but nothing could hide the muscles beneath his clothes.

He laid the axe against the stump and her throat dried up as he strode toward her. She never had a problem talking, something her family teased her about, but after last night, an inexplicable wave of shyness rolled over her. Normally she knew where a relationship was headed but with Scott, he hadn't given much of an indication of what he wanted *from her*. Well, other than he obviously wanted *her*. And she definitely wanted him right back. Last night was like a thrilling tease of what was to come.

"Did I wake you?" he asked as his hands settled on her hips. His deep voice sent a thrill like she'd never experienced rushing through her.

She shook her head and slid her arms around his waist. She wasn't going to tell him that he'd woken her up when he was doing something incredibly sweet.

He dropped a kiss on her forehead then on top of her head as he pulled her tight against him. He smelled fresh and earthy and like something else she couldn't quite define. Whatever it was, she wanted to bottle it up. "I made coffee," she murmured against his chest.

"Sounds good . . . Go on a date with me tonight, Michaela," he spoke against her hair and that voice sent another zing zipping through her at lightning speed. Right to the heat already building between her legs. There was something about the way he said her name and the way he sort-of asked, sort-of ordered her to go out with him. There was almost a note of nervousness to it. Which was crazy. He couldn't possibly think she'd say no. Everything about his voice simply made her knees go weak.

"Okay," she murmured.

"I get off work at five so I'll pick you up at six if that works."

"That works." She nodded against his chest, savoring the feel of his muscles. She could hardly wait to feel his skin beneath her fingers and mouth. He'd continued exploring her body last night but hadn't allowed her to touch him much. She wasn't sure why but that was going to change tonight. Because she was all about giving back to him.

"I want to get some of this wood inside your house before I head to work." His voice sounded slightly strained, as if leaving her was the last thing he wanted to do.

Good, because the feeling was mutual. And she loved that she affected him as much as he did her. He might not have let her touch him everywhere last night but he certainly wasn't immune to her. His rock-hard erection pressing against her abdomen was proof enough of that.

* * *

Scott rolled out from underneath the Mercedes he was working on to find Daniel leaning against the hood, staring down at him. And he had a big shit-eating grin on his face.

"What the hell's the matter with you?" Scott asked.

"Nothing. You got plans tonight?"

"As a matter of fact, I do." He still couldn't believe what had happened with Michaela last night. Or that the sexy woman wanted more from him.

"You finally ask Michaela out or something?"

He narrowed his eyes. "Why?"

Daniel shrugged and his grin grew even wider. "We're behind on two vehicles and instead of getting pissed, you've been grinning like a fool all day."

Damn, he hadn't realized he was that obvious. It was only a date. It wasn't as if she'd committed to something more. Scott pushed up and slid the roller back under the car with his foot. "We might be going out."

"About damn time," Daniel muttered.

Scott ignored his friend's words. He and Michaela were from different worlds. Not that she was a snob or anything, but he didn't see her committing to anything long-term with someone like him. He knew that getting a taste of her and losing her would likely kill him, but he didn't care. She was worth it. "It's just a date."

"Don't take her somewhere pretentious. She hates that shit."

Something akin to jealousy jumped inside him, clawing at him. He didn't like it. "How do *you* know?"

Daniel grabbed a clean rag and started wiping at the grease on the exposed part of his arms as they headed toward the front office. "I heard her bitching to Darby last week about pretentious assholes."

"Oh right." They might have grown up in the same town but they'd never crossed paths until recently. Scott was five years older than Michaela so they'd never been in school together. The day after he'd graduated high school, he'd joined the military. It had been that or jail. He'd been on a dangerous path to destruction and he'd known that if he didn't clean up his act, he'd have ended up just like his old man. Well maybe not exactly like him but he'd have likely been a screw up. Back then he'd known who the Miller family was but he hadn't run in the same circles as Michaela. And her two brothers were a couple years younger than him too. He felt uncomfortable asking Daniel but decided he didn't have anything to lose. "Where do you think I should take her?" He'd planned on going to the only French restaurant in town. Not his style, but he'd figured it was something she'd like. Now he wondered if that was the best choice.

"Cook for her."

"What?"

"Man, I've got two sisters. Women like that shit. Cook something special for her. It'll show you put some thought into tonight."

"You ever cook for the women you . . . date?"

Daniel snorted. "Hell, no. If I cook it sends the wrong message. You, however, want more than what I'm looking for." His friend said it as fact—and he wasn't wrong.

Unlike Daniel, he'd never done the casual thing. And cooking wasn't a bad idea. Now he needed to make a stop before showering and cleaning all the grime off him. Scott grabbed his car keys from the hook inside the office. "You mind locking up?"

"Course not, boss. I'll see ya, Monday."

Anticipation hummed through him as he walked to his 1967 Mustang. The last time he'd been so excited over something was when he'd bought this car. But that feeling didn't compare to the thought of getting to spend more time with Michaela. Even though he knew it was destined to end between them, how he felt at the moment, it was hard to care.

Before Scott made it to his car, the sheriff pulled into the parking lot.

"Son of a bitch," he muttered under his breath. Scott leaned against his car and folded his arms across his chest while waiting for the sheriff to park. Because he was clearly here to see him—or to harass him.

The sheriff parked next to him then slammed his door with a lot more force than necessary. He rounded the car and faced Scott. "Where are you off to? Seeing *Michaela* again?"

Scott gritted his teeth. He didn't like the inflection of the sheriff's voice. Hell, he didn't like that bastard even thinking about Michaela. Instead of answering the question or letting the old man know it bothered him, Scott shrugged. "Why are you here?"

His blue eyes narrowed. "I know what you did. Don't think you can hide behind sweet Ms. Miller for long. Sooner or later you'll slip up and I'll catch you."

"What the hell are you talking about? It's not my fault your nephew is a fuckup, so don't go pretending I did anything to him."

The sheriff took a menacing step in his direction. "Fuckup? You're one to talk. How long you think that pretty little thing is going to stick around? To her you're just some trailer trash she's using for a good time and soon enough, you won't have her for an alibi."

Rage popped inside him. As he clenched his fists at his side, Scott bit his tongue because if he didn't, he'd deck the sheriff. Which might be exactly what the old man wanted. Hell, then he could arrest him for assaulting a member of law enforcement. If there was one thing the Marine Corps had taught him, it was to control his temper. He couldn't control every situation but he could damn sure get a handle on himself. After taking a deep breath, his vocal chords loosened. "Is there anything else you need from me, Sheriff?"

The sheriff's jaw ticced as he shook his head. He looked almost disappointed. Maybe he had wanted Scott to hit him. "No, but I've got my eye on you."

Scott resisted the urge to roll his eyes as the sheriff got back in his car. Unless he planted evidence on him, Scott wasn't going to let some small town sheriff get the best of him. He might have screwed up as a kid but he was a law-abiding citizen and the only crime he was guilty of was occasionally speeding.

CHAPTER SIX

Terrance tapped his finger against his steering wheel, watching as O'Callaghan pulled out of his parking lot. He'd thought for sure the guy would deck him. That would have put him exactly where Terrance had wanted him.

Once O'Callaghan was gone, he pulled out of the parking lot and headed in the other direction. He was already off his shift and it was time to go home. He might not like the mechanic, but he wasn't going to follow him or give him a reason to file a complaint.

Terrance had used less than politically correct tactics before but he'd never crossed any big lines and he wasn't about to start now. Not even for his nephew.

No, he'd be retiring soon, probably in time for the next election. He was getting older and his wife had been after him to take more and more time off. Which was fine with him. He was ready to enjoy his retirement years with her.

When his phone rang, he glanced at the caller ID and answered. "Hey, Shirley." His sister-in-law rarely called him. Usually she called his wife because they were close so this had to be an emergency of sorts.

"Hey, Terrance. You, uh, talked to Frank lately?"

"Saw him yesterday. Everything all right?"

She cleared her throat delicately. "I don't know. I stopped by the house today and found Lyla picking up some of her things. Seems as if she moved out a week ago . . . Did you know they'd separated?" Her voice shook as she asked.

He sighed and swung a left at the next side street. Frank should still be at work. "No, he didn't say a word. They been having problems?"

"Well, she'd mentioned something the last time we had lunch, but I wasn't sure if it was just typical problems. You know how these kids are today. Most marriages don't last after a few years."

He grunted in agreement.

She continued. "I've called him a few times but I think he's ignoring my calls. He'll talk to you though."

"I'm pulling into his shop now," he said resigned to face this.

"Thank you. I know he respects you."

After assuring Shirley he'd check on her son, he disconnected the call and got out of his car. The place looked closed but the open sign was still lit up and Frank's car was out front. Once inside, Terrance didn't bother calling out his nephew's name.

Rounding the main desk in the lobby, he glanced at the calendar and stack of work orders. Some of them were weeks old with notes that Frank needed to call them back. It looked like he was getting work. Maybe not as steady as O'Callaghan, but he was getting it and just not following through. The knowledge annoyed him.

When he didn't find Frank in the garage, he strode past the three pits and opened the office door on the other side of the area.

Frank was leaned back against his chair, eyes closed, snoring softly with a half-empty bottle of Scotch on his desk.

Damn it.

Terrance rubbed a hand over his face and grabbed the car keys hanging on the holder by the door. He'd have to take him home and get him into a bed.

Now he was starting to wonder if maybe his nephew was having more problems than he'd imagined. And whether they had more to do with him being drunk and passed out at work, actively driving customers away, as opposed to a competitive company. Because who could blame customers for not wanting to do business with Frank when he wasn't even working.

* * *

Michaela stared at her reflection in the mirror and critically assessed herself. She wore a dark blue wraparound sweater that brought out her gray eyes. Growing up she'd hated the unusual eye color, especially combined with her bright red hair, but as she'd gotten older her hair had darkened to a soft auburn and she'd learned to embrace her uniqueness. Looking like everyone else was boring.

The doorbell chime set her pulse pounding. She zipped up her four-inch boots over her slim-fitting jeans, grabbed her purse and hurried down the stairs. She was actually going on a date with Scott. Her eyes widened after she swung the door open. Scott stood on her front porch carrying two large paper bags. Leafy greens and a baguette protruded from one of them.

"What's this?"

"I thought I'd cook for you."

The last guy she'd gone on a date with had taken her to the most expensive restaurant in town, then proceeded to harass their server the entire meal. It had been so embarrassing. She'd ended up leaving an extra tip to compensate. Not that she worried Scott would be rude to anyone, but this was refreshing. "Here, I'll help." She reached out for one of the bags, but he sidestepped her.

He chuckled. "I got it," he said and headed toward her kitchen.

She shut and locked the door before sliding her boots off. If they were going to have an evening in, her feet weren't going to suffer needlessly. Her heart skipped a beat when she entered the kitchen and found him with his back to her emptying one of the paper bags. He looked so at ease and *so right* in her kitchen, it scared her a little.

For so long she'd dated what she considered cookie-cutter men—similar education and background to her own and usually know-it-alls when it came to politics or religion—it was so refreshing to be with a man like Scott. He spoke when something needed to be said, he didn't talk about how great he was and from the sneak preview she'd gotten last night he was a giving lover. There was nothing soft about him either. His dark sweater stretched across his broad shoulders, showcasing muscles she'd like to run her fingers over. Well, her fingers and her mouth. She'd been fantasizing about it for the better part of the year.

She covered the distance between them and leaned against the counter so that she faced him. "What are you making?"

He pulled out a bag of fresh, uncooked shrimp. "Shrimp Alfredo over pasta." He paused suddenly, looking almost panicked. "Are you a vegetarian?"

She grinned and shook her head. She loved seafood too much. "No. Do you want me to make the salad?"

"Sure."

It was obvious he was comfortable in his own skin, but something told her his unease came from her. And that surprised her. She was cute in the girl-next-door kind of way, but she wasn't stunning or model gorgeous. The knowledge that she made him nervous was a bigger turn on than she could have imagined. But she really wanted him to get over it. Last night on the porch swing he'd lost all traces of that discomfort as he'd intimately stroked her.

"So what's the story behind your snake tattoo?" she asked.

He glanced over his shoulder while he filled one of her pots with water. "I was young and stupid."

"You don't get off that easily. I've seen your other tattoos too." As soon as she said it, she wanted to take the words back. It sounded as if she'd been watching him. Which she sort of had been, but she didn't necessarily want him to know that.

His dark eyebrows lifted curiously. "Is that right?"

She shrugged and tried to act casual but could feel her cheeks heat up. At that moment, she hated having the coloring of a redhead. "I've seen you working out on occasion." When he grinned, she continued defensively. "It's not my fault you practically strip naked while doing it."

He shook his head and transferred the pot to the stove. "You're one to talk. Over the summer I thought I'd have a heart attack watching you prance around wearing those little bikinis."

So he *had* noticed. She smothered a smile. "I do not prance," she said as she plucked a wineglass from one of her cabinets. Without looking at him, she continued. "And you never answered my question."

"I don't remember a question."

"Your tattoo?" She uncorked the same bottle from the night before and poured a small glass.

His shoulders lifted slightly. "There's no big story. I was in Recon when I was in the service and one night me and my team got matching tattoos. It's sort of related to a mission we went on and managed to survive."

"I think it's sexy," she murmured into her glass.

"And I think you're sexy." His blunt declaration silenced her. Before she could respond, he placed his beer on the counter and stalked across the room to where she stood by the fridge. The way he moved was all sleek predator, making her knees go weak.

He took the glass from her hand and placed it on the counter somewhere behind her. The dark look in his eyes was enough to make her melt. Reaching out, he cupped her jaw and just stared at her. As if he wanted to eat her whole.

She swallowed as their gazes locked. Something gleamed in his eyes. She wasn't quite sure what it was, but it was completely primal. This was a different side to Scott. One she very much wanted to get to know.

Being dominated in the bedroom was something she craved but she'd never found a man to completely satisfy her. She didn't want to get spanked or anything like that, but the thought of letting go of all her control made her body temperature spike about a thousand degrees. She was pretty sure Scott would have no problem fulfilling all her needs.

"What are you thinking right now?" His hold on her cheek tightened slightly.

"That I'd like to skip dinner and go right for dessert." The words came out as a throaty whisper. She couldn't believe she'd actually uttered them, but there was no going back now. Because this was so happening tonight.

He dropped his hand and for a split second, disappointment curled through her until she realized what he was doing. Scott turned the stove off then shoved the cold foods into her refrigerator. Without glancing at her, he headed for the back door. She started to ask what he was doing when he spoke.

"Wait for me in the living room. I'm going to grab some extra wood." Even though his voice was slightly strangled, the words came out as a subtle order.

And she liked it.

Her heart beat erratically as she made her way to her living room. Instead of sitting on the couch, she grabbed a couple pillows from her loveseat and stretched out on the alpaca rug in front of the fireplace.

They were probably moving *way* too fast, but it was hard to care. Normally she dated a man for months before thinking about sleeping with him. And even then, she usually got too bored with them before taking that next step. With Scott, it was all she seemed to think about. Sleeping in the same bed as him last night but not actually having sex had been torture. She wasn't sure how he'd managed to exert so much control. She jumped when she heard the back door shut.

A few seconds later, he rounded the corner into her living room. His dark eyes zeroed in on her face and what she saw there caused her panties to dampen. She'd never seen so much raw need from anyone before.

He knelt in front of the fireplace but was silent as he started the fire. Moments later a bright blaze illuminated the room with flickers of orange and gold. She pushed up on her knees and sat facing him as he moved back toward the rug.

"Do you know how long I've wanted to get you in this position?" he asked quietly. Sincerely. They were sitting directly in front of one another and she desperately wished he was inside her instead.

"What took you so long?"

His jaw ticced, but he didn't answer. Instead, he reached for the tie on her wraparound sweater and slowly pulled the bow undone. She shrugged out of it and let it fall behind her. She started to reach behind her back, but he stopped her. Without touching her anywhere else, he reached around her and unhooked her bra.

As the skimpy covering slid down her arms, he made a guttural sound that sent shock waves straight to the ache between her legs. Her nipples hardened under his intense gaze.

Unable to take his heated perusal of her body anymore, she scooted forward and reached for his sweater. "Now it's your turn."

Immediately he stopped her. He covered her hands and held them in place by the bottom hem of his sweater. Last night he hadn't taken his sweater off either. Pausing, she stared at him, waiting. She'd seen him working out before and she couldn't imagine why he'd be embarrassed to take his clothes off. Not with a body like his.

He stared at her, and she was under the impression that some invisible battle raged in his head. Finally he let go of her and lifted the sweater off himself. When he was bared to her, she gasped when she saw the pale circular scars covering most of his stomach. There were so many of them. She'd only seen him from a distance so she'd never have been able to see the markings. It took a second to realize they were likely old cigarette burns. Like really *really* old. She didn't know much about his family other than his mom was dead and his father was a drunk. If she had to guess, he'd gotten the burns from his father. A protective rage jumped inside her that anyone could hurt their child like that.

It bothered her that he thought she'd care about something as superficial as scarring. Leaning forward, she pressed her lips to his chest then continued a trail down the muscular planes of his stomach. He shuddered under her kisses and fisted an unsteady hand through her hair. She loved the way he gave a little tug.

"Michaela." His voice was ragged.

She lightly raked her teeth over his skin. When she neared the top of his pants, his stomach muscles bunched. Without looking up, she pressed a light hand against his chest again.

"Lay back," she murmured against him.

Again he paused, but he did as she said. Once he was flat on his back with a pillow under his head, she grappled with his button and zipper. After she pulled his dark jeans down, her throat seized as his erection sprang free. He was bigger, thicker than she'd guessed. For some reason, she wasn't surprised he went commando. Instead of pulling them all the way off, she only pulled the jeans to his knees, giving him limited mobility.

When she glanced at his face, all she saw was need and hunger. Keeping her eyes on him, she slowly bent down until she hovered over his thick length. She swiped her tongue up the full measure of his shaft. From bottom to top.

A bead of come glistened at the tip so she swirled her tongue around the mushroom shaped head, licking it up. His hips jerked unsteadily as she fisted the base of his cock and took him fully in her mouth. She let out a throaty hum of pleasure.

"Fuck, Michaela." He leaned up and grabbed her by the shoulders with trembling fingers. The trembling surprised her more than anything.

"What?" She stared at him in confusion.

"I've waited too long for this. I don't want to come in your mouth. Not this time." Lightning fast, he hooked his hands under her armpits and flipped her on her back.

All the air whooshed from her lungs as she watched him shimmy out of his jeans then tug hers off. He moved like a man possessed. The heat from the nearby fire was nothing compared to the raging flames burning inside her. Now there was nothing between them except her panties. She noticed that his hands shook as he retrieved a condom from his discarded pants.

She wanted to sheath him just so she could touch him again, but he ripped it open before she could protest. Kneeling in between her legs, he clasped the thin straps of her lacy panties and slid them down her legs. An involuntary shiver escaped as his gaze zeroed in on the juncture between her spread legs. She'd never felt more exposed—or turned on.

Scott's cock jumped as he traced his finger along Michaela's slit. She was soaking wet, something that gave him immense pleasure. It felt too surreal to have *Michaela* in front of him like this with nothing between them. The firelight reflected off her delicate features and that gorgeous red hair of hers. She looked like a goddess stretched out before him. Soft yet lean in all the right places. It was clear how much she worked out at her yoga studio.

For once in his life, he wished he was a little more charming. He'd never needed words in the bedroom but he wanted to somehow tell her how beautiful she was, how much it touched him that she'd kissed his hideous scars. Everything he thought of sounded stupid though. Silence was definitely the best option.

He pushed a finger inside her and just like the night before, her tight sheath locked around him in a vise like grip. She was wet but so tight. And soon it wouldn't be just his finger. That thought made his hips roll involuntarily.

"Ahh," she let out a small moan.

"You like that?" he whispered, not wanting to break the intimacy of the moment.

"Yes," she hissed as he pushed deeper inside her.

He pulled out with the same slow precision. As he dragged his finger against her inner walls, she arched her back and made little moaning sounds that tested all his restraint. His balls pulled up painfully tight and he wanted nothing more than to pound into her. But she wasn't ready just yet and he didn't want to hurt her.

When she fisted the throw rug underneath her, he pushed another finger inside her and kept both of them still as he leaned down and kissed her clit. The bud peeked out from her swollen lips begging to be licked.

He swept his tongue over it and her hips jerked against him. He couldn't contain the chuckle that escaped. The woman was so reactive. Like a firecracker. He still couldn't believe how fast she'd climaxed last night. After witnessing the expression on her face the first time he'd made her come, he definitely wanted a repeat performance. Soon.

Licking her clit, he increased the pressure with his tongue and moved his fingers again. In and out. He kept the rhythm steady. And just like that, her inner walls started contracting around his fingers. It was so sudden, he hadn't been expecting it.

"Scott." She moaned his name like a prayer.

He didn't want to feel her coming around his fingers though; he wanted to feel her tight sheath milk his cock. Sitting up, he repositioned himself at her entrance. Before he could move, she shifted and impaled herself on him. He almost exploded from the shock. Her mouth formed a perfect O as he filled her to the hilt.

Shit. A zap of awareness shot through his entire body, his spine tingling as pleasure filled him. She wrapped around him like satin. He leaned forward as he started to move inside her, wanting to feel her breasts against his chest. The contractions he'd felt around his fingers tripled around his cock as she reached the peak of her orgasm.

She reached around him and dug her fingers in to his back. Hard. The slight pressure of her nails bordered on pain but it only added to his pleasure. She was so lost in her climax.

The hardened points of her nipples rubbed against him and even that got him hot. He'd never been so aware of every part of his body. And he'd never thought of the missionary position as anything special but right now, he didn't want to do it any other way. He wanted to see every expression on Michaela's pretty face.

Her eyes were half-open as he continued thrusting into her. His cock was ready to explode but he made himself hold out. When she wrapped her legs around his waist and locked her ankles behind his back, he lost it. Crying out, he let the climax rip through him until the waves of pleasure subsided.

He drove into her until his hips were blindly thrusting against hers. Instead of completely collapsing on top of her, he held himself up with his elbows. He knew he should roll off her and give her room to breathe but her legs were still wrapped around him and her fingers were still firmly embedded in his back, as if she didn't want to let him move either.

A mischievous smile spread across her face and she ran a hand through his hair, stopping when she cupped the back of his head. "We could have been doing this for the past seven months," she murmured.

"Don't remind me. I've been walking around with a permanent hard-on since I moved in." He grinned as he covered her mouth with his. As their tongues danced with each other, her words sank in and he couldn't help but wonder if she might be interested in something more serious.

CHAPTER SEVEN

Michaela groaned and pushed her plate away. "I can't eat another bite. That was so good." They'd finally gotten around to cooking dinner. Well, Scott had cooked. She'd watched and drank wine. Her favorite type of "cooking". If he kept this up, she wasn't letting him go.

"You've got to keep your strength up because we're just getting started tonight." The small grin that spread across Scott's face made her heart squeeze. He so rarely smiled and it made her happy that she was able to pull one out of him.

She started to say something else when his cell phone buzzed. Again. Other than the sounds of them eating, her house was quiet so she knew the buzzing had to be his phone. Her cell was in her purse.

"I'm sorry." He reached into his pocket and started to turn it off, but she reached across the table and threaded her fingers through his free hand.

"That's the second time. It might be important." She owned a business too so she understood getting calls at random hours. Usually it was someone calling out because of a sick kid or because they were sick themselves.

As if on cue, it buzzed in his hand again.

He gave her an apologetic look but she shook her head. "Seriously. Answer it, it's okay."

Scott frowned at the caller ID then slid his finger across the screen. "Hello... This is he... What? Are you... No. I can't... I'll be there tomorrow. I don't ..." He glanced at her and motioned that he was going to step outside.

Even though she was curious about his conversation, she took the opportunity to put their plates in the dishwasher. There was a ton of shrimp and pasta left over so she stored it in a plastic container. As she was putting it into the fridge, the back door opened and Scott stepped back inside. "Is everything okay?"

His expression was a virtual mask and his nod was curt. "It's fine. Here, let me help." He started to move for one of the dirty pots, but she placed a hand on his forearm and stood between him and the stove.

"What's going on?"

His Adam's apple bobbed up and down once. "That was the hospital. My father died tonight. Hit and run accident."

With his words, it was as if all the air was sucked from the room. Her eyes widened. "What?"

His jaw clenched once and he shrugged, but the action didn't come off as casual as she guessed he wanted. "I need to claim the body but it can wait until tomorrow.

That son of a bitch never…" He trailed off and shook his head. "Forget about it. I don't even know why I said anything."

Staring into his dark eyes, her heart twisted at the grief she saw there. Her parents had both passed away. Her mom from cancer, then her father had passed months later from heart failure despite being reasonably healthy. She'd always thought he simply couldn't live without her mother. But she'd loved them both dearly and had been heartbroken without them. Even though it was obvious there was no love lost between them, the man had still been Scott's father. She didn't want him to have any regrets.

Her hand tightened on his arm. "Let's go now. Come on. I don't want you doing this by yourself later."

He frowned at her. "Michaela—"

She could hear the argumentative tone in his voice so she sidestepped him and headed for the hallway. "I'm just going to put on my shoes." Without waiting to see if he followed, she strode from the room.

Seconds later his heavy shoes sounded along the wood floor. While zipping her boot up, she glanced up at his approaching figure.

"It would be pointless to argue with you, wouldn't it?" he asked, his voice low.

"Yep." Whether he admitted it or not, that he'd even asked meant he probably didn't want to go by himself.

She stood and grabbed her coat and purse from the rack by the front door. "I'm ready when you are."

* * *

"Mr. O'Callaghan, I'm sorry for your loss but the truth is, your father wouldn't have made it another six months. I don't know if he'd told you but his liver was failing." Dr. Benson leaned casually against the counter at the nurses' station.

No, his father hadn't told him because they hadn't talked in months. The only time his father contacted him was to ask for money, booze, or to bitch at him for being a waste of space. The last time he'd talked to him he'd been at a sports bar with Daniel—and his dad had been passed out in a motel he didn't recognize and needed help. Even though he'd hated the old man, he'd still gone to get him. Scott had offered so many times to get him into rehab, but he'd always declined. "What did the police say? Were there any witnesses?" Scott glanced over at Michaela sitting on the small plastic seat in the hospital waiting room as he spoke to the doctor and his heart skipped a beat. He couldn't believe she'd wanted to come with him.

"Not that I'm aware of. Detective Martinez was down here earlier. He said he'd be calling you."

"What about Sheriff Hill?" Even saying the old man's name left a bitter taste in Scott's mouth.

The doctor's mouth pulled into a thin line. "Haven't seen him around." By the subdued tone, it sounded as if he didn't have much respect for the old sheriff either. That was interesting. The doctor cleared his throat and held out his clipboard. "If you'll just sign this last form, I can release his belongings."

Belongings? Scott wasn't sure he wanted anything from his father, but he scribbled his signature at the bottom of the paper anyway. After he did, the doctor leaned over the counter and retrieved a small brown bag. Scott risked a glance inside. Just a lighter and a couple small bottles of half-empty whiskey. Big surprise.

"This is it. Just so you know, Morton's Funeral Home handles most arrangements but if you plan to let the city bury him—"

"I'll call Morton's in the morning." He wasn't going to have a funeral but he'd bury his father next to his mother. Even though it pained him to do so, he knew it would be what his mother wanted. He shook the doctor's hand then headed toward Michaela.

She stood when she saw him. His gut clenched as she strode toward him. Taking her to the hospital was the last thing he'd ever wanted to do and definitely not on their first date. Even in death his father was fucking with his life. But when she'd offered, he simply hadn't been able to say no. Her offer had been completely sincere.

Silently, she linked her arm through his as they headed down the hallway. Her boots clicked loudly against the linoleum. The rhythmic sound was strangely soothing.

Cool, refreshing air rushed over them the second they stepped outside. A car horn blasted in the distance and an ambulance siren wailed louder and closer as they headed across the parking lot. It felt too surreal that his father was dead. Guilt gnawed at him that he'd ignored the last few messages from his father. He didn't owe him shit, so why should he even care?

Scott had been ignoring the existence of their relationship for the past couple years. He'd given the man money for food when he'd needed it, but that was it. When it had been clear he'd never be interested in rehab, Scott had needed to cut mental ties. Hell, his father was lucky Scott had even talked to him at all. After his mother had died, he'd become a punching bag to Mickey O'Callaghan. And an ashtray. Couldn't forget that. His body wouldn't let him. He'd spent four torturous years under that man's roof until the day he'd turned eighteen and joined The Corps. Hell, even his teenage rebellions had been partly just to survive. Each car he'd stolen all those years ago was so he could get to the grocery store and buy food for him and the old man.

"Want me to drive?" Michaela's quiet question jerked him back to reality.

He glanced down at the petite redhead who'd gotten under his skin in a bad way and shook his head. "No, but thank you."

"You okay?" she asked as he held open the passenger door for her.

"I'm fine. I promise." He dropped a quick kiss on her lips before shutting the door and rounding to the driver's side.

Maybe he wasn't exactly fine, but he'd deal with it. He'd lived the past couple years like he didn't have a father. Now he wouldn't have to pretend anymore.

Twenty minutes later, Michaela played with the strap of her purse as Scott held open her front door and let her step inside. He hadn't said much on the ride back from the hospital. Not that she'd really expected him to.

She risked a quick glance at him as he shrugged out of his coat. His face was once again a mask. He might try to hide his pain but she knew better. More than anything she wanted to do something to make him feel better.

"I'm going to make sure your back door is locked and everything's put up," Scott said before disappearing down the short hallway.

She started to follow him then changed her mind. After slipping off her boots and socks, she shimmied out of her jeans and left them in the middle of the foyer. As she ascended the stairs, she stripped her top off, her bra, then her panties.

The trail led directly to her bathroom.

She turned the shower to almost-steaming hot then stepped under it. Closing her eyes, she stepped under the pulsing jets. As the water rushed over her, the steam rose, filling the enclosed space and creating an even more intimate atmosphere.

Without opening her eyes, she knew when she wasn't alone any longer. If Scott was anything, he was certainly stealth. Like a jungle cat. What she'd thought of as shy before was really his quiet nature.

The man was a hunter and she very much enjoyed being his prey.

But the presence in the shower changed subtly and she knew he was there. Big, strong hands settled on her hips. She smiled when she felt his warm lips press against her neck but she still didn't open her eyes. She simply enjoyed the sensation of his mouth on her skin.

Scott shifted closer so his thick length pressed against her stomach. She could feel the cover of the condom and grinned. *Good.*

"Tell me what you want." His mouth was close to her ear now. The warm breath sent a shiver curling through her.

If her nipples weren't already rock hard, they would be after a dose of his deep voice. She wasn't sure what it was but whenever he spoke, her nipples woke up and paid attention. Maybe because he didn't do it often. Or more likely because something about the way he talked rolled over her like warm butter.

"I'm waiting," he whispered.

"Touch me."

"Where?" Now he whispered into her other ear. She hadn't even heard or felt him move. Damn, the man was good.

She opened her eyes and found herself staring at a wall of muscle. Rivulets of water streamed over his hard muscular chest, creating little rivers. She leaned forward and kissed one of his nipples. "Between my legs," she whispered against his skin.

He cupped her mound but didn't make a move to do anything else.

"Are you being intentionally difficult?" she murmured.

"Tell me *what* you want." His finger moved slightly against her folds but he didn't make a move to penetrate her.

Fine. He wanted to know. She'd tell him. "I want you to fuck me until I can't walk. My body's so hot right now I feel as if I could explode. Make me come, Scott. Long and hard."

Her words set him off. He growled something incomprehensible against her neck before kissing and sucking on her soft skin. His teasing was harder this time and sure to leave marks. She smiled at the thought.

Reaching out, she braced one hand against the wall and the other against the shower door. Her head fell back as he continued a trail of kisses across her neck down to her breasts.

When his teeth clamped over one of her nipples she let out a tiny cry. It didn't hurt, but it bordered on painful. And she liked it. The sensation was new and exciting. He continued licking and teasing the hard bud with fast strokes.

Nothing about tonight would be gentle and she felt primed for it. She'd been waiting for a man like Scott for too long. He might be quiet but he knew how to take charge when it counted. And he certainly knew how to touch her.

He grabbed her by the hips and pressed her flat against the wall. She wrapped her legs around him and using his shoulders for support, she held on to them to balance herself.

Scott didn't even seem bothered by her weight. The muscles corded tightly in his neck were the only giveaway that he was straining at all.

"Kiss my other one," she moaned.

Without wasting time, he switched breasts and feasted against her sensitive skin. Her breasts were heavy and aching with need. But the ache between her legs was greater. She squeezed her thighs around him and pushed up.

The tile was cool against her back but it didn't matter. A raging volcano burned deep inside her and the only way she was going to find release was with Scott's help.

She could almost swear he read her mind when he reached between them. Without testing her, he cupped her mound and pushed two fingers deep inside her.

The intrusion was more than welcome. Arching her back, she pushed her breast deeper into his mouth. He continued his wicked assault on her nipples, switching back and forth using his teeth and lips.

His fingers moved inside her with urgency. So close to climax, her muscles clamped around them but she wanted his thick length inside her and nothing else.

"Your cock." It was the only two words she could manage.

Luckily they were descriptive enough. All the muscles in his arms and chest pulled taut as he shifted his weight.

With his gaze firmly on Michaela's, Scott grabbed her hips and thrust her down onto him. Her mouth and eyes widened at the same time as his cock filled her to the hilt. Her inner walls molded around him, imprisoning him in her tight body. If he moved too much he was afraid he'd come. That couldn't happen yet. She needed her release first.

He pulled out almost all the way then thrust back into her. Her fingers tightened on his shoulders but she didn't take her gaze off him.

Those perfect lips of hers parted slightly and her pale eyes seemed to glow with hunger. Rolling his hips, he thrust into her again.

And again and again.

The harder he pushed, the harder she panted. Each lungful of air she pulled in was labored and uneven.

She was so close he could feel it. With every thrust she was running toward that edge. He didn't know why she wouldn't just jump. Her inner walls clenched around him in a death grip. The woman was primed. She simply needed the nudge.

"Let go. Come for me, Michaela." His command set her off.

She bucked against him and pushed completely off the wall. With a cry, she wrapped her arms around his neck and he kept pummeling into her. Her inner walls spasmed around his cock and her cream rushed over him.

Her orgasm was hot and fast.

Finally he could let go. Surrender to her the way his body demanded.

Reaching lower, he clutched her ass and gripped it hard. Her skin was soft but tight. Something in the back of his brain told him to slow down but he couldn't. His hips moved against her as if they had a mind of their own.

His cock wanted—demanded release. And Michaela was the only one who could give it to him. He buried his head against her neck and thrust one more time.

Long and hard, he came. His climax seemed to go on forever. Unable to control himself, he groaned. "Michaela." The sound of her name was loud in the small, tiled enclosure.

Finally, when he caught his breath, he pulled his head back. His knees were weak but he held her up.

Michaela smiled, a small, knowing smile. The corners of her lips tugged up but she didn't let go of her embrace around his shoulders. "My legs are pretty weak. I think you're gonna need to carry me to the bed."

Chuckling under his breath, he shut off the shower and stepped out with her still attached to him.

This woman was like an addiction. He knew he was going to sink deeper and deeper into her web but he couldn't stop himself. Even if she broke his heart, he didn't *want* to stop himself. Every second he spent with her would make it worth it.

CHAPTER EIGHT

Scott's grip around Michaela's shoulders tightened. The sexy vixen was naked and stretched out on top of him. And unfortunately for him, she was completely passed out. After the last bout of sex, he guessed she'd be out for a few more hours despite the sun having already risen. Luckily he didn't have to work today and neither did she. That meant a lot of uninterrupted time between the sheets if he had anything to say about it.

Slivers of orange light streamed through the blinds in her room, coating the bottom half of her bed. His cock was practically ordering him to wake her up, but he tempered his desire and loosened his hold.

Easing her off him, he pulled the comforter higher up until it reached her neck, then he grabbed the quilt draped across the antique rocking chair in the corner of her room and covered her with that. The heat in her house was sketchy at best so he tugged on his jeans and sweater and headed downstairs to put more logs on the fireplace.

He needed to take care of some stuff around his own house later, but he didn't want to leave hers. And that scared the shit out of him. Getting too attached to her was stupid, but he couldn't seem to help himself. They were good together in the bedroom and if he could convince her they were good out of it, maybe they'd have a chance.

After starting a pot of coffee, he peered into her fridge. With the exception of the leftovers from last night she had mainly girl food. Yogurt, fat-free milk, sushi and a bunch of vegetables. At least she had eggs and bacon. He could make breakfast with that.

As he pulled out the carton of eggs, he froze at the sound of her front door unlocking then opening. Male voices trailed down the hall and into the kitchen. *Who the hell had a key to her place?* A surprising jolt of jealousy punched through him. Whoever it was, they weren't trying to be quiet so he wasn't worried about an intruder. Nonetheless, he grabbed a knife and inched toward the archway that exited into the hallway.

He peered around the corner then froze when he saw Jake and Thad Miller midway down the hall, heading his way. When they spied him, all talking ceased as they stared at him. They did not look happy. *Shit.* He didn't have a sister but if he did, he doubted he'd like to find some guy making himself at home at her place in the early hours of the morning.

Jake, the oldest, stepped forward. "Scott O'Callaghan? You plan on carving us up with that?"

He glanced down at the knife still clutched in his hand, then back at them. "Ah, no." When they didn't make a move, he motioned behind him with his free hand. "There's a fresh pot of coffee on." He retreated into the room and quickly placed the knife back in its rack.

Leaning against the counter by the sink, he waited for them to enter the room. The two brothers had the same auburn hair as Michaela but they didn't have her eyes. Instead, Scott found himself staring into two dark—and pissed off—gazes.

"What the hell are you doing here?" Thad demanded heatedly.

Jake nudged him and cleared his throat. "I think what my brother means is . . . shit, what the hell are you doing here?"

There was no beating around the bush. "Your sister and I are..." *What were they exactly?*

Jake's eyes narrowed. "Are?"

"We're none of your business." Michaela stepped into the room wearing those tight yoga pants that left nothing to the imagination and a loose Duke sweatshirt. Her tousled hair and swollen lips left little doubt what Scott was doing there with her. She crossed the room, slid her arm around his waist and nestled tight against him. Her small action loosened the vise around his chest. At least she wasn't ashamed to be seen with him.

"What are you guys doing here so early?" she asked.

"You needed help putting those shelves up, *remember*?" Thad's voice was thick with sarcasm.

"Right." Her cheeks tinged a delicate shade of pink. "I forgot," she mumbled.

"Michaela, let me talk to your brothers alone," he murmured quietly, but he wasn't asking.

She stared at him in surprise, no doubt because of the subtle command in his voice, but he didn't care. She nodded, then skirted past her brothers without another word.

Once he heard her ascending the stairs, he took a few steps toward them. "Listen, I don't have a sister and I don't know what the protocol for this is so I'm just going to say it. I like your sister . . . a lot. Whatever needs fixing around here or whatever she needs taken care of, I'll be handling from now on."

Almost in sync, both their gazes narrowed slightly. "For how long?" Thad growled protectively.

"Until she gets tired of me." The words were out before he could stop himself, but it was true. Michaela wasn't the kind of woman a man willingly walked away from. If things ended between them, it would be her choice.

Thad took a menacing step toward him but Jake grabbed him by the arm. "We'll see you later, Scott."

"What the hell are you doing?" Thad muttered to his older brother.

"Don't be an ass. Come on." Jake looked at Scott as he shoved his brother toward the hallway. "You and I are gonna talk later."

Scott nodded. "I don't doubt it."

He waited until he heard the front door shut then he headed up the stairs. Her bedroom door was slightly ajar. He nudged it open to find the comforter thrown back and Michaela stretched out on the sheets completely naked.

"Damn, woman," he murmured as his cock hardened.

"I'm glad you got rid of them. Those stupid shelves can wait." With a wide grin on her face, she propped up on her elbows. The action pushed her breasts out farther. Her nipples hardened as he drank in the sight of her stretched out. Finally he tore his gaze away and focused on her face. A small, knowing smile tugged at the corners of her lips. As if she knew exactly how much she affected him.

His skin heated under her roving gaze. Without pause, he grabbed a condom from his back pocket and shucked his pants and sweater. At the rate they were going, he was going to need to invest in Trojans. He ripped open the packet as he stalked toward the bed. When he reached the foot, he sheathed himself. His cock jerked when Michaela wordlessly spread her legs a few inches wider.

That small tuft of red hair covering her mound drove him crazy. She trimmed it into a little triangle and the rest of her surrounding skin was silky smooth.

For how he felt, he wanted to pound into her until he was completely sated. Though he doubted that was even possible.

He'd tasted practically every inch of her, but he wanted to take her from behind this time. "Turn over." His voice was uneven and he was afraid if he touched her first, he wouldn't be able to even talk.

Her pale eyes darkened with desire and her lips parted as she flipped over and pushed up on to all fours. Glancing over her shoulder at him, she wiggled her ass playfully.

Biting back a groan, he ran a palm over her smooth skin. She shuddered under his touch and scooted back a couple inches.

Kneeling on the bed behind her, he kissed her lower back as he reached between her legs from behind. He trailed his finger over her slit and teased her entrance. No surprise she was wet. Without testing her first, he slid two fingers inside her. She gasped and moved against his hand.

It would be so easy to get her off in this position, but he wanted to be inside her. He withdrew his hand and held on to her hips tightly. Instantly he had to force himself to loosen his grip.

"Please do something." Michaela clenched the satiny sheets beneath her. Her breathing came in short, shallow gasps.

"Do what?" he asked as he leaned forward and kissed the curve of her spine. When he did, his cock rubbed against her opening, but he didn't push in any farther. He wanted to hear her say exactly what she wanted. He hadn't thought he needed any talking in the bedroom but hearing Michaela say what she wanted him to do was a turn-on all by itself.

"You know what I want."

"Say it," he murmured.

"Fuck me." The words tore from her throat in a scratchy whisper.

That's all he needed to hear. In one fluid movement he thrust into her. Her inner walls clasped tightly around him. It molded and fit perfectly.

The desire to please her more than himself frightened him. He'd always enjoyed pleasing a woman but this was different. She was different. Everything he was starting to feel for her scared the shit out of him because he didn't quite understand what was happening to him. Michaela was like his 67' Mustang. He'd worked a long time to get her and the thought of losing her left a hole inside him. He could get used to waking up to Michaela every morning. Much too easily.

Sliding his hands up her waist and over her ribs, he settled his palms until he cupped her breasts. In this position they felt fuller, heavier in his hands.

He'd found out in the shower she liked it when he got a little rough. When he captured her nipples between his fingers and pulled on them, she moaned and pushed back against him. His abdomen muscles clenched painfully as he held back from coming.

Michaela was so close to climaxing, it wouldn't take much to push her over the edge. It seemed all Scott had to do was touch or look at her and she lit on fire. Just like that. She was ready to burst into flames of desire. When she'd woken up this morning and he hadn't been in her bed, disappointment had immediately surged through her.

She started to move against his cock, but he dropped one of his hands from her breast and wrapped it around her waist.

He held her firm so that her ass was firmly against him. He leaned down toward her neck. Pushing her hair over one of her shoulders he nipped her ear. "You don't move until I say so."

A ripple of hunger trilled across her neck at his order. With the exception of her erratic breathing, she stilled at his words. Hell, she'd do anything the man asked her to as long as he kept that thick length inside her.

Her inner walls throbbed with the need for release but he seemed intent to take his time. Not that she minded. They'd had so much sex in the past couple days it was hard to wrap her mind around the fact he'd simply been her sexy neighbor a few days ago.

The hand wrapped around her waist splayed across her abdomen before dipping lower. He barely grazed her clit, teasing her.

She clutched the sheet tighter and he had the gall to chuckle. Heat gathered low in her belly. He had to know how close she was and he was taking his sweet time getting her there. Well, payback would be just as fun.

Mercifully, he pinched her nipple and her clit at the same time. The dual actions sent a zing of awareness to every nerve in her body. When he stroked her clit with more insistency, he dropped the hand caressing her breast and gripped her hip with it. Then, he thrust into her.

Hard.

Over and over, his cock thrust into her with a wild urgency that left her breathless.

Behind her she could hear him whispering things about how gorgeous and sweet she was and how long he'd been waiting for someone like her. The words were what pushed her over the edge. Scott, *who never talked,* was saying the most beautiful things anyone had ever said to her.

As his cock pistoned into her and his finger rubbed over her aching bud, she convulsed and clamped tighter around him until spasms racked her entire body. The climax hit hard and fast, rolling over her like a powerful tsunami.

Before she was finished coming down from her high, Scott latched on to both her hips and cried out her name as he came. His thrusts became more rough and uneven with each stroke until finally he collapsed on top of her.

Her breasts, still sensitized, pressed against the cool sheets. Groaning, he rolled off her. Using a small reserve of energy, she turned over to face him.

After a few minutes passed, she traced a finger over the tattoo on his upper arm. It was of dog tags that simply said USMC in the middle. "Do you regret getting any of these?"

He shifted so that he was on his side and faced her. "No. Why? You don't like them?"

"I already told you I think they're sexy." She couldn't contain a grin. Before meeting him she'd thought tattoos were stupid, but now . . . she'd most definitely changed her mind. "So why'd you get out of the military anyway?"

He shrugged and draped his hand across her waist. "Eight years was enough. I'd never planned to stay in more than four, but when the time came to reenlist, so many of my friends were staying in, I did too."

"Do you keep in touch with them?"

"Hell yeah. Some are still in The Corps, but most of them are in some sort of law enforcement or overseas contract work now. I talk to at least one of my buddies every other week."

"And you never thought about going into law enforcement?"

He snorted and pulled her closer. "Not even once. I love working on cars and I make my own hours."

"Good. You should love what you do." She scooted even closer so that their bodies were flush against each other and she draped her leg over his waist. "Listen . . . my brother's girlfriend is throwing a surprise party for him next weekend and I was wondering if you'd want to go with me." Even though he wasn't exactly moving, Scott's entire body stilled under her touch. She swallowed back her disappointment. Maybe it was too soon to be thinking about something like that. They hadn't made any promises to each other and for all she knew, he wasn't thinking in the same relationship terms she was. "Never mind, it's probably too fast. I—"

His hold on her hip tightened. "I want to go. Are you sure your family will want me there, though?"

There was a strange note in his voice. One she couldn't place her finger on. She frowned at his question. "Why wouldn't they? Because of this morning? I'm an adult, something my brothers know. Your being here just surprised them, that's all."

He cleared his throat. "That's not what I meant. We don't exactly run in the same circles."

She bit her bottom lip as his words sank in. "What the hell does that have to do with anything? My family doesn't give a shit about that and neither do I. You run a successful business in our community and you served your fucking country for nearly a decade." Her voice rose with each word and she wasn't sure why she was getting so worked up. She wasn't angry at him, but she was pissed that he'd actually think that.

"Don't get all twisted up, Michaela. I was just saying—"

"I know exactly what you were saying and I don't like it."

To her surprise, he grinned. Actually *smiled*. A real one. It softened his entire face and made her insides melt. That adorable little dimple deepened. "If that's all it takes to get you to curse, I'm going to have to rile you up more often. I like it when you talk dirty."

"I curse plenty," she muttered.

Chuckling, he cupped her cheek, then took her mouth in a dominating, heated kiss. Whatever had been running through her head quickly dissipated when his tongue stroked over hers. She wasn't sure where their relationship was headed, but she'd never felt more at ease with a man in her life.

CHAPTER NINE

"I can't believe you managed to tear yourself away from that sexy man," Devon said on an over-exaggerated sigh.

Michaela swiped the small chocolate garnish from Devon's chocolate martini and popped it into her mouth.

"Hey!"

"That's what you get for calling her man sexy," Darby said, snickering behind her own martini. Devon, Darby and Michaela were all at a high top table in one of the newer local restaurants. And it was happy hour. "Even if he is. According to our brother, he thinks it's about time Scott got some balls and asked you out."

This was all news to Michaela, but she kept her mouth shut, knowing she'd learn more that way. Monday night was typically their girl's night out after work, which meant martinis and sometimes a movie. It was the only night that worked with their schedules. Darby was a kindergarten teacher so most nights worked for her and she hated Monday's because of the staff meetings and needed to blow off steam after work. Devon

96 | SAVANNAH STUART

owned a bakery and Tuesday mornings were her late day.

"Come on, I want details. It's been forever since I've gotten any action," Devon moaned again, in that over-exaggerated way that Michaela loved.

Next to her Darby snorted. "Liar."

To Michaela's surprise, Devon's cheeks tinged bright pink.

"What? Who are you seeing?" Michaela demanded. Devon was never shy talking about her dates.

"No one." She shot a glare at her twin. "Snitch."

Darby just grinned wider.

"Why is this the first I'm hearing about this?" Michaela called or texted with the two of them practically every day.

"He works for—Ow!" Darby yelped as her sister kicked her under the table.

"If you say anything I'll tell Michaela about—"

"Fine," Darby grumbled, bending down and rubbing her leg.

Michaela shook her head, used to their banter. They'd all been friends since they were in kindergarten and the twins were always finishing each other's sentences. The women were beautiful, and looked like freaking pinup models from the fifties. If she didn't love them, she'd probably hate them a tiny bit. But they were both ridiculously sweet, if a little maddening at times.

And she didn't have the heart to tell either of them that she was pretty sure she knew exactly what they'd both been about to say. Scott had mentioned something about seeing Devon leaving with one of his guys for lunch today so she was probably dating someone who worked for Scott.

And Michaela was ninety-nine percent sure Darby had a crush on one of her brothers. The last time the quiet twin had been around Thad she'd acted weird and flustered, which was unusual for her. "Talking to the two of you is a test in patience. Just saying."

"You still haven't given us anything juicy," Devon complained, clearly not through with her grilling.

Not that Michaela minded. She took a long sip of her drink before eyeing her friends. "Fine. The *multiple* orgasms are insane. The man is a freaking machine and I've barely gotten any sleep the past few days and I so don't care. Oh, and Thad and Jake showed up Saturday morning while Scott was making coffee at my place way too early for me to have a neighbor over. Happy?"

"Multiple orgasms . . . bitch," Darby muttered, a teasing grin spreading across her face.

"And that's enough drinks for you," Devon said, sliding her sister's drink across the table so that it sat in front of her.

For the next couple hours they talked, shared drinks and ate way too much food until finally Michaela said goodbye. She loved her girl's nights but she could admit to herself that she was seriously ready to get home to Scott.

Outside on the sidewalk, she wrapped her scarf tightly around her neck before fishing her keys out of her purse. She'd only had one martini hours ago so had no problem driving. She'd left her car parked at her yoga studio since it was only a couple blocks over.

She'd only taken a couple up the street when she spotted the sheriff and his wife headed down the sidewalk, the older woman's arms linked through his. She didn't care for the man but she actually liked his wife. So, Michaela knew she couldn't be rude. *Damn it.*

Passing by them, she gave them a smile and a polite hello, even if it was forced, and wasn't surprised when they stopped her since she knew Lois.

"Michaela, so nice to see you out," Lois said with a smile.

"You too, Lois. You're looking great." The older woman was petite and in really good shape for any age. She took Zumba classes twice a week with Michaela and she knew the woman jogged regularly.

"Thank you, sweetie. So are you, as always. I'll be seeing you on Thursday won't I?"

Michaela nodded. "I'll be there." Taking a deep breath, she forced a smile as she faced Terrance Hill. She hated confrontation. It ranked right up there with public speaking, but she needed to get something off her chest and felt compelled to do it now. "Sheriff Hill, I know you have a problem with Scott, but he's a good man. He served his country and he runs an honest business that's putting money back into this community. He's nothing like his father."

Under the street lights she could see the sheriff flush as he nodded. He mumbled something she could barely understand then said goodbye, practically dragging Lois down the sidewalk with him. She could hear Lois asking him what Michaela had meant.

Feeling a huge weight lift from her shoulders, she continued on to her car. She'd said what she needed to say. Someone needed to stand up for Scott.

* * *

Terrance steered into the driveway of his nephew's house, his fingers clenched tightly around the wheel. "We should have called first," he murmured to his wife.

Lois shook her head. "He's been ignoring you since you stopped by his shop and took him home. Someone needs to talk some sense into him."

At dinner he'd told her everything that had been going on. Not that he'd actually had a choice. After what Michaela had said in front of Lois, he'd had to tell his wife.

And Lois was pissed, to put it mildly. So here he was because he did not like his wife angry at him. The more he'd been chewing on everything that had happened, the more he wondered if Frank had been lying about the break-in. The fact that he hadn't filed an insurance report could be chalked up to his high deductible, but it could also be because Frank hadn't wanted to commit insurance fraud.

Damn it, he hated doing this. He left the engine running and unsnapped his seatbelt. "I'll be back in a little bit."

His wife smiled sweetly. "I'm not going anywhere."

When he reached the door he started to knock but realized it was open a couple inches. And someone was shouting inside. Frowning, he took a step forward but paused when he realized it was Lyla and Frank shouting at each other. He definitely didn't want to hear this, but he stayed put when he heard glass breaking.

"Damn it, Frank. Breaking my favorite mug isn't going to make me stay. We're through, why can't you just understand that?" Lyla's voice was pleading.

"Because I'm not good enough for you anymore?" His voice was sullen and slurred.

"I need someone I can count on."

"Someone more successful!" he shouted.

Terrance shifted from foot to foot, uncomfortable hearing any of this. But he wasn't sure he should go.

From the sound of things, it was possible the argument could escalate. He'd never known his nephew or Lyla to be violent but he also hadn't realized that they were breaking up. Or broken up, it seemed.

"That's not what I said."

"But it's what you mean! You want someone like that O'Callaghan who's not a fuckup like me, right?"

"Oh my God, Frank. We've been over this. This is about me and you. I'm tired of having to take care of everything. I'm surprised you even notice I'm leaving!"

Frank replied but it was too quiet for Terrance to hear. After a few minutes of them talking too low, Terrance backed up and headed to his car. It seemed as if they'd both calmed down and he didn't want to embarrass either of them. He slid into the driver's seat and backed up, keeping his lights off.

"What's going on?" his wife demanded.

"Not sure." He reversed then parked across the street and quickly relayed what he'd heard. He wasn't leaving until he was certain Lyla was gone and things hadn't re-escalated between the two of them. A few minutes later Lyla came out, a box in her hands. She shoved it into the trunk of her car then left. Instead of checking on his nephew he decided to head home. He needed to talk to Frank when he had a level head, not right as he was drunk and coming off a fight with his wife.

Damn it, he hated being wrong, but now he really wondered if he'd been blind to Frank's problems and potential lies. Maybe . . . he'd misjudged Scott.

CHAPTER TEN

One Week Later

Michaela slipped her coat off and hung it on her coat rack. "That wasn't so bad, was it?" she asked Scott.

He grinned and hooked his coat up next to hers. "Your family's nice. Loud, but nice."

All her cousins had been incredibly welcoming to her new "boyfriend". She'd tried to tell them not to call him that, but they hadn't listened. After spending every lunch break and every night together over the past week, she assumed she and Scott were headed in that direction but didn't want to get ahead of herself. Of course, her brothers were still wary of him. Scratch that, Thad was still wary. Jake had taken a fast liking to him. Well, as much as an older brother could to the guy sleeping with his little sister. At least he'd been incredibly welcoming, which meant everyone else followed his lead. That was all she could ask for.

"You sure my cousins didn't bug you too much?" Cheri and Delia, two of her younger cousins had latched on to him like Velcro. They'd wanted to know all about his tattoos, being in the Marines and how fast his car went. The ten-year-old twins had shot one question after another at him like machine gun fire.

He shook his head and slid his arms around her waist as he pulled her close. "They were fine. Stop worrying."

"I know, but they're my family. I *know* how annoying they can be." It wasn't that she was exactly worried he'd be scared off by them, but she'd come to learn how quiet and private he could be. The exact opposite of her relatives.

He cleared his throat. "You're lucky, Michaela. I wish I had that many people who cared about me."

Her throat tightened at his words. She wasn't sure if there was a proper response to that so she simply hugged him back. As far as she knew, his father had been his only living relative and Scott hadn't even had a funeral for him. Of course he'd had him buried, but he hadn't wanted to do anything big. Not that she blamed him now that he'd opened up to her about what a bastard his father had been.

Scott's grip around her tightened and she knew they were going to end up in her bedroom within the next sixty seconds, but the jingle of her phone pulled them apart. She fished the cell out of her purse and cringed when she saw the caller ID. It was her Aunt Katherine, mother of the twins. "I'm gonna grab this now or she'll keep calling all night until I pick up."

Scott dropped a kiss on her forehead. "I'll put some logs in the fireplace."

She flipped the phone open. "Hey, Aunt Katherine."

"Hey, darlin'. I hope I didn't interrupt *anything.*" She giggled loudly and Michaela couldn't smother her smile.

"Are you drunk?"

"I'm a little tipsy, but don't tell Dan," she mock-whispered.

Michaela rolled her eyes. As if she were actually going to call up her uncle and nark out her *grown* aunt. "What's going on?"

"Nothin'. I just wanted to find out what was going on with you and Mr. Tall, dark, and sexy. The girls have done nothing but talk about their new Uncle Scott."

Panic jumped in her gut. "*Please* stop saying that. And you better tell the rest of the family to cut it out too." She loved her aunt, but she was one of the biggest gossips in town.

"Why? It's serious, isn't it?"

Yes. "No, we're not serious so just leave it alone."

"Well, you're an idiot then, girl. If I had a man like that—"

"Good Lord, how drunk *are* you?" Her aunt was always talking about how much she loved her husband. In annoying, intimate details.

"Oh please. I love my husband, but that doesn't mean I can't appreciate a little eye candy every now and then. I was just calling to let you know the family likes him and approves of him."

"Well I don't give a shit if they approve of him." And she didn't. She liked him and that was all that mattered. Of course she wanted her family to take to him, but it wasn't a prerequisite or anything. She made her own decisions and she wanted Scott in her life. Or more like needed him. She'd gotten so used to seeing him every day it was a little scary.

"Don't get your panties in a twist, Michaela."

She sighed and sank onto one of her kitchen chairs. "I'm sorry, it's not that. I..." She wasn't sure how to word her feelings without sounding pathetic. While she was excited about her new relationship with Scott, she also didn't want to jinx it by thinking about the future too much. For all she knew, he was a commitment phobic. Though she sort of doubted it considering how much time they'd spent together. Still, she didn't want to mess up the first good relationship she'd had in years because he got the idea she was marriage crazed. "Just tell every-one to keep their mouths shut about him and me and cut out that 'uncle' stuff. I don't know how serious it is, okay?"

Scott stood frozen in place as he listened to Michaela's conversation. He hadn't meant to eavesdrop but when she'd said they weren't serious, his feet had turned to lead weights. He'd thought . . . well whatever it was, he'd been wrong.

An icy fist clamped around his heart. When he heard her say goodbye, he backtracked down the hall. Instead of heading for the living room, he grabbed his coat from the coat rack.

"What are you doing?" Michaela asked as she walked down the hall. A frown marred her pretty face.

"I got a call from Daniel. Emergency down at the shop." If he went home, she'd know he was lying. It was a total chickenshit thing to do but he needed some distance.

"On a Saturday night?" There was a trace of disbelief in her voice.

"I'm sorry. I'll call you."

She tucked a loose strand of hair behind her ear and eyed him warily. "Okay."

Before he could change his mind, he left. He didn't make a move to kiss or touch her because he knew if he did, he'd want to stay. And that would only be more painful. The front door shut behind him with a quiet click.

As he drove into town, he didn't bother with the radio. Maybe he should have stayed and talked to her, but he wasn't sure what to say. He'd planned to tell her tonight that he wasn't planning to sleep with or see anyone else and he wanted to make sure she was on the same page. They hadn't actually discussed a future, but he'd never felt about anyone the way he did about her.

And she didn't think it was serious. *We're not serious... I don't give a shit if they approve of him.* Her words echoed around in his head like a broken recording.

"Fuck!" He slammed his hand against his steering wheel. He was a fucking pussy. What they'd shared over the past week *was* serious. There was no doubt in his head. He knew she felt the same way. He was just letting his old bullshit and insecurities get in the way.

When he pulled into the parking lot of his shop, he immediately kicked his car into reverse. He'd run out on her like an asshole and she deserved an explanation. And hell, if she wasn't serious about him then he needed to know now. As he started to leave, he noticed a light bouncing around through one of the windows of the main storefront. "What the..." It was from a flashlight. The realization hit him like a punch to the stomach. Someone was in his garage.

He immediately turned his car and the headlights off. For a brief moment he thought about calling the police but quickly brushed it aside. He doubted Sheriff Hill would do much to help him. And hadn't he mentioned a break-in at his nephew's place? Maybe the old man had been telling the truth. This could be the same guy.

Quietly, carefully, he opened and shut his car door, then raced toward the side of the building. Whoever this was wouldn't know the layout of his store so they were virtually working blind with the exception of that flashlight. His heart pounded a little faster as he edged toward one of the side EXIT doors that led to the main garage. After unlocking it, he ducked inside then crouched behind one of the high end cars they'd kept over the weekend.

The hood was popped open and Scott knew he hadn't left it like that. *What the hell was going on?* He thought he heard a rustling sound coming from the office area so he inched toward the rear of the vehicle and peered around.

When he did, light flooded the main garage and he found himself staring down the barrel of a gun.

"What the hell are you doing, Frank?" Scott kept his voice steady and even as he stood up.

Frank Hill stood four feet away by one of the main light panels with a weapon in hand—a .40 Smith and Wesson by the looks of it. And that hand was shaking something fierce. "You weren't supposed to be here."

"Neither are you." Scott couldn't keep the wry note out of his voice.

The man rubbed his free hand over his face. Looked as if he had three day old stubble and his eyes were red rimmed and glassy. "Shit, shit, shit."

"Talk to me, Frank. What's going on? You need money?"

"I don't need your charity!" he screamed.

Yeah, but he had no problem stealing. Scott took a small step toward him. He'd had enough training that he could disarm Frank. If he didn't get shot first, of course. "Talk to me, man. This isn't about money, is it? Something else is going on."

Frank nodded unsteadily and the gun wavered again. Scott took the opportunity to close another few inches between them. "Lyla...she left me. Said she wanted to be with someone she could count on. Someone more successful."

Out of the corner of his eye, Scott saw a flash of unmistakable red hair duck behind one of the counters in the outer office area. His entire world tilted on its axis. What the hell was Michaela doing here? Only a glass wall separated her from a man with a gun. He forced himself not to look in her direction. He couldn't let this piece of shit know anyone else was here. "So you were planning to steal from me?"

Frank shrugged and had the decency to look a little apologetic. "I was going to sabotage a couple of your customers' cars, get some business driven my way. That's all, I swear."

The fact that he was telling him meant he likely wasn't planning to let him go. Scott could see Michaela inching toward the glass door toward them. Now he wished he'd called the cops. Or hell, never left her house in the first place. If he hadn't, she wouldn't be here. Instead, they'd be tangled up in her sheets.

"What's the plan now, Frank? No one's been hurt. You need to put the gun down and leave."

"Why? So you can call the cops on me?" he spat.

"What am I gonna tell them? You haven't done anything. It's my word against yours and the sheriff is your uncle. No one would believe me anyway. Just put the gun down and leave. I'll forget this ever happened. Everyone deserves a second chance."

"Second chance," he muttered.

In that moment, Scott knew Frank was seriously contemplating putting the gun down. His options were clear. Unfortunately, at the same time the realization hit him, a loud police siren wailed in the distance.

"You son of a bitch! You called the cops!" He swung the gun in a wide arch.

Scott was still too far away to get to him. He moved a couple inches closer and shook his head. "How could I have done that? And *why* would I have done that? I came here alone tonight to get some paperwork done. If I'd wanted to call the cops, I'd have let them come here and arrest you and never set foot in my place. That siren isn't for us." Or he really hoped it wasn't. If the cops showed up, he'd be screwed. And Michaela . . . he couldn't even think about what could happen to her.

Frank scrubbed a hand over his face. "That makes sense."

A crash inside the main office jerked both their attention away. Scott knew it was his only opportunity. Frank swung his gun toward the office and Scott saw red. Covering the rest of the distance, he threw himself at Frank.

Frank was faster than he imagined. He whipped back around, but Scott went straight for his weapon hand. He knocked him off balance then broke his trigger finger. After that, taking the gun was easy.

"Owww!" Frank howled in pain as he backed away from Scott.

Tucking the gun into his waistband, Scott advanced on the other man and decked him. By nature he wasn't violent, but this piece of shit had swung a loaded weapon toward Michaela. That alone deserved a beating. His fist connected with Frank's jaw with a crunch and he slumped to the concrete like a crumpled piece of paper.

"Scott!"

He turned to find a wide-eyed Michaela rushing toward him. The glass door slammed shut behind her and her boots clacked against the concrete floor. Before he could move, she'd flung her arms around his neck and nearly knocked him over. "Oh my God! Are you okay? I called the cops and my brothers when I saw the broken glass out front. I didn't know what else to do. What did that maniac want with you? Are you sure you're okay?"

Despite the situation, he chuckled as she fired questions at him. He pulled his head back but kept his hands firmly on her hips. "I'm fine, sweetheart. Are you okay?"

"Me? You're the one who had a gun pointed at your head."

"It's over."

She ignored him as a river of unexpected tears streamed down her cheeks. "This is all my fault."

His gut clenched. *Shit.* Not tears. Anything but *her* tears. "Don't cry. Please, don't cry."

"I can't help it. I know why you left. You overheard that stupid conversation I had. I didn't realize it until you'd gone. That's why I followed you." Her voice was thick and unsteady.

"I was an asshole. I shouldn't have left like that. If you want to take things slower, we'll—"

"No, you stupid man! I don't want to take anything slower. I just thought all that talk from my family would scare you off so I told them to back off."

His heart turned over in his chest. Cupping her jaw, he swiped at the stray tears still tumbling down her soft cheeks. "Scare me? I love you, Michaela." The words slipped out before he could think about what he was saying.

Her pale eyes widened. "*What?*"

His throat dried up as she stared at him with that soul searching gaze. Maybe he should have waited. *No.* He loved her. It was a simple thing and it felt liberating to say it to *someone.* He'd never uttered those words to a woman other than his mother before and instead of feeling foreign, it felt right. So right it terrified him.

"I love you too," she whispered.

"Don't say it because—"

Her grip around his neck tightened. "Don't tell me what to do, Mr. Bossy. I pretty much realized it earlier tonight when you let my cousins jump all over you like you were their personal jungle gym. You sealed the deal when you told my Aunt Celia you liked her awful macaroni and onion salad. Blech."

"That's all it took?" he murmured. He'd been half in love with her since the day she'd showed up at his front door all those months ago carrying a plate of cookies. She'd looked so hot in that skimpy summer dress all he'd been able to think about was pushing it up and taking her right on his front porch.

She sniffed in a haughty manner that had his cock standing at attention. Of course it was the wrong time, but his lower body didn't care.

Flashing red and blue lights caught his eye through the front office. He sighed and looked back at her. "Looks like the cavalry is here."

"Good, the sooner they get that jerk out of here, the sooner we can get back to my place." All traces of her earlier tears were gone as her voice dropped an octave.

He wrapped his arms around her and squeezed her tight against him. Heading back to her place sounded like heaven. If he had any say over things, sooner rather than later, they were going to get a place together. And then, he'd see about convincing her to spend forever with him.

* * *

Michaela tugged her coat off before Scott put his car in park. They'd left her car at his shop and after hours of filling out paperwork and answering questions down at the police station they were finally back at her place.

And she was insanely turned on. It was ridiculous. She should be exhausted but all she wanted to do was jump Scott. From the heated looks he'd been giving her during the drive back, he felt the same.

Scott unstrapped his seatbelt, then hers. Before she realized what he intended, he lifted her and pulled her on top of him.

Avoiding the gear shift as he tugged her over, her knees settled on either side of him and sunk into the black leather bucket seats. There wasn't much room but it made this hotter.

As their lips and bodies meshed together, she tried to wrap her mind around everything that had happened that night. A few weeks ago Scott had simply been her neighbor. Her very sexy neighbor she was forced to only fantasize about. Now she got to do whatever she wanted to him.

When she'd thought she might lose him tonight, it was as if the bottom of her world had fallen out.

He showered kisses on her lips and jaw until he located the sensitive spot at the nape of her neck. Good Lord, the man knew exactly what she liked and where she liked it. A pent-up moan of ecstasy escaped, and her hands fisted into his thick hair. He could take her from zero to hot-and-ready-to-go in milliseconds. One of his hands slipped under her top and started working its way up.

"Will you go on birth control? I want to fuck you without any barriers," he whispered against her neck. His words came out almost as a growl.

Something warm bloomed deep inside her core at his question. She pulled back and looked into his face and saw need. Pure and raw. He might want her physically, but he needed her just as much as she needed him. It scared and excited her at the same time. "Okay."

They were so close she could see where his iris met his pupil, though his eyes were so dark it was almost impossible to distinguish the line.

Her mouth was full of cotton, and she couldn't contain the tremors racing down her spine straight to her core. She felt as if she needed to say something else but now wasn't the time for talking.

"Strip."

A low gasp escaped. "What?" Her question came out as a breathy whisper.

In the dim light of his car, his eyes darkened, taking on a feral appearance. "Don't trust myself not to rip your clothes."

Her stomach clenched at the demanding tone of his words. Involuntarily her panties dampened. His sexy scent had taken over the car. Spicy and masculine, he permeated everything in the enclosed space. Right now it felt as if they were the only two people in the world and that was more than fine with her.

As Michaela slowly peeled off her top, Scott felt as if his heart would stop. It didn't seem to matter that he'd seen her naked a couple dozen times, his cock ached and pressed against his jeans, begging to be unleashed. Begging to push deep inside her.

And she wasn't wearing anything underneath. His gut clenched when he realized she wasn't wearing a bra. His body demanded to feel her skin against his and the only way that was happening was if he managed to get his clothes off.

But first, he wanted her out of her jeans. He needed to see more of her. All of her. He grappled with her button and zipper and then managed to shove her pants to her ankles. She still had her boots on, which limited her mobility. The thought of her at a slight disadvantage was insanely hot.

As quickly as humanly possible, he stripped off his shirt then unzipped his jeans before quickly rolling on a condom. He didn't even bother with boxers around her. It was pointless.

Threading his hands through the curtain of her hair, he cupped the back of her head and sought out her mouth with his. As he swept his tongue across hers she clutched onto his shoulders. He loved the way she held on to him as if her life depended on it. Each time they made love she gripped him with a fierce need that humbled him.

The energy humming through her was practically rolling off her in waves it was so potent. With his free hand he slid his hand around her waist, then strayed to her ass. She still wore her thong but the scrap of material was basically non-existent. He hadn't bothered pushing it down with her jeans when all he needed to do was shove it to the side.

Moaning, she rubbed her breasts against his chest. The woman made wild, purring sounds as she tangled around him.

For once, he needed to restrain her. "Michaela." He pulled his head back and spoke softly against her cheek.

"What?" she panted.

"Do you trust me?"

That stilled her. She bit her bottom lip nervously but nodded. "Of course."

"Put your hands behind your back." He didn't tell her why or what he was going to do.

She stared at him for a moment then nodded and did as he said. Blindly he reached behind the bucket seat and felt around on the floor until his hand clasped what he wanted.

When he pulled the small bungee cord up, her eyes widened but she didn't move. His cock felt like a club between his legs but he forced himself not to blindly thrust into her the way he wanted. Not yet.

He secured her wrists against the steering column. The action pushed her breasts out farther and with her legs spread wide around him and her hair tumbling wildly around her face, she looked like a goddess. A wet dream come to life.

Without taking his gaze off hers, he pushed her thong to the side and strummed her clit with his finger. Just a light teasing. Each time he stroked her, she jerked against his hand. Her hips continued to roll against him but he wanted to drag this out. Give her more foreplay.

He leaned forward and teased her nipple with the same light pressure he was giving her clit. It was enough to drive her crazy but not enough to give her what she wanted.

When she let out a frustrated moan, he pushed one finger inside her, testing her slickness. She was tight, but wet. He pushed another finger in and she opened herself wider for him. Well, as wide as she could. Her jeans created a kind of manacle around her ankles.

"I don't want foreplay. Not now. I just want to feel all of you. *Please.*"

That's what he needed to hear. The desperation in her voice sent an arrow straight through him.

He withdrew his finger and pushed his hips up. When she started grinding against him, he completely buried himself inside her, filling her as deep as he could go.

She let out a tiny cry, and he momentarily stilled. She was wet and willing but still tight. It didn't matter how many times he had her, the woman was always a perfect fit. As she moved against him in a desperate rhythm, he gripped her hips and thrust upward.

He held on to her so hard he knew he'd leave bruises but he didn't care. He was marking her. She was his and tonight had only confirmed his feelings for her.

It was almost impossible to believe he was here with her. Not long ago he'd been trying to figure out a way to simply say hello to her without breaking into a nervous sweat. Now he knew they were meant to be together. All that social class bullshit had just been something for him to hide behind.

The damn woman had such a tight hold on him, he wondered if she realized how much power she had over him. Slight tremors shook his entire body as he restrained himself from coming. As soon as he'd entered her, all the muscles in his body had pulled taut.

When her breathing started coming in short, rapid gasps and her inner walls started contracting around him tighter and tighter, he knew how close she was.

The gorgeous woman was moving fast and frantic and before he realized it, she surged into orgasm. Her thighs tightened around him as she came and she leaned back against the steering wheel. It shook underneath their pounding.

Wild, explosive, and red-hot. She was like a package of dynamite.

As she cried out, he let himself go. Grabbing on to the steering column behind her so he wouldn't bruise her skin even more, he drove into her until he was completely spent. Even after he'd started to soften, his cock thrust into her with blind desire.

Somehow he forced his hands to work and he untied her. With a sigh, she fell against him, letting her head rest on his shoulder. "Wow."

He grinned against her hair. He couldn't think of a word more perfect to describe it. "Wow is right."

The smell of sex hung heavily in the air, and even if he might be ready to go again, she definitely wasn't.

He'd pounded into her hard and fast, and even though she'd been dripping wet, he had a feeling she might be a little sore. "I didn't hurt you, did I?"

She shook her head and her red hair tickled his nose. "You could never hurt me."

And he wouldn't. Hell, he couldn't. She meant too much to him.

Four months later

For what felt like the hundredth time that day, Scott patted his pants pocket. The small box was still there.

"That's the last of them," Michaela said, entering the kitchen as he shut the door to the dishwasher and started it.

Her family had come over for dinner that night and the big crew had been loud and boisterous, as usual. He knew she sometimes got frustrated with them, but he also knew she adored every one of them.

"You love them," he murmured, moving around the kitchen toward her.

"True. And I love you," she said. Taking him off guard, she crossed the rest of the distance between them and jumped him, wrapping her legs around his waist.

He couldn't hear that enough. Brushing his lips against hers, he started to deepen the kiss when she shifted against him and pulled back a fraction. Frowning, she reached down and patted his pants pocket. "What's this?"

Well, hell. Moving to the island, he set her down on one of the chairs. He'd planned to do this later tonight when they were both naked in front of the fireplace. But to hell with waiting. He felt as if he'd been waiting for this woman his entire life.

Sweet, smart, and sexy, she was better than he ever could have imagined. And he wanted to spend the rest of his life with her. He just hoped she felt the same way.

Reaching into his pocket, he started to go down on one knee. By the time he'd pulled the blue ring box out of his pocket she was squealing in delight and throwing her arms around his neck.

Laughing, he buried his face against her neck and inhaled. Even her scent drove him crazy. "Do I get to ask the question first?"

"Yes! And the answer is yes! And you better be freaking proposing or I'm going to be so embarrassed." Her eyes widened in panic as she looked at him.

"Marry me." He released his grip from around her and opened the small box.

The diamond twinkled under the kitchen lights and Michaela threw her arms around him again, crushing her mouth to his.

As their tongues danced together, he took her left hand in his and slid the engagement ring on her ring finger. He wanted the whole damn world to know this

woman belonged to him. Because he was never letting
her go.

Thank you for reading Tempting Alibi. I really hope you enjoyed both stories and that you'll consider leaving a review at one of your favorite online retailers. It's a great way to help other readers discover new books and I appreciate all reviews.

If you liked Tempting Alibi, turn the page for a sneak peek of more of my work. And if you don't want to miss any future releases, please feel free to join my newsletter. I only send out a newsletter for new releases or sales news. Please find the signup link on my website: http://www.savannahstuartauthor.com

CLAIMING HIS MATE

L auren Hayes shoved a wayward strand of hair under the knit cap she wore as she slid up to the outside back wall of the quiet, two-story house. The black cover over her hair had nothing to do with the chilly October weather. Right now she was all about blending into the shadows this cold fall night. Which meant dressing in all black, like a sneaky burglar.

Because she was about to do something stupid. Incredibly stupid. She inwardly berated herself.

There was no turning back now. Shifters were notorious gossips and word had spread through the grapevine that Grant Kincaid, alpha of the Kincaid wolf pack in Gulf Shores, Alabama was on a honeymoon.

With his new human mate.

That by itself had shocked the shifter world. Kincaid's father had been a brutal bastard—before he'd died. A shitty alpha who'd hated anyone who wasn't supernatural. Or at least that's what Lauren had heard.

The current alpha was two hundred years old and she was twenty-five so it wasn't as if they'd ever run in the same circles. She'd also heard Grant wasn't like his father and from the brief meeting she and her pride had with him six months ago, she had to agree that he seemed pretty decent.

Even if he was a stubborn ass who refused to give her family back what was rightfully theirs. Now that the alpha was out of town, she and some of her pridemates had decided to break into his house.

To steal from him.

Maybe steal was a bit of a stretch, she thought as she moved against the side of the house. Wind whipped around her, sending another shiver racing through her. She was simply taking back something that belonged to her family's pride. She had to remind herself of that. Her sister was getting married in two weeks and the broach the elder Kincaid had taken from her family almost a hundred years ago was supposed to have been a wedding gift when the oldest Hayes daughter got married. The piece of jewelry had been in their family for centuries. Well, the jewels had been. Three, four-carat—*colorless*—diamonds and a handful of emeralds had been passed down from oldest daughter to oldest daughter in some form of jewelry ever since. When Lauren's mother had received a necklace from her mother, she'd had the jewels put into a broach instead.

And Lauren desperately wanted to give it to her sister Stacia as a wedding gift. She deserved it.

Since Lauren was one of the few shifters on the planet who could mask their scent from other shifters, vampires and pretty much all supernatural beings, she'd been more or less volunteered for the job by her cousins. She also had a knack for breaking into places. Not that she was normally a thief. Her cousin Tommy, however, was. When she'd been twelve he'd taught her a lot of tricks, including picking locks and hotwiring cars. Her parents had been so pissed when they'd found out. After she stole back what was rightfully theirs, she bet they'd be glad she had those extra skills. Of course they'd be angry at her for doing this, but she'd known if she told them they would have ordered her not to. She figured it was better to do this then beg forgiveness later.

She had a few pridemates waiting a mile away in case she ran into trouble, but they had to stay out of sight unless she called them.

Right now they were all on Kincaid territory. Didn't matter that it was a touristy beach town right on the Gulf Coast and that humans had no idea a shifter pack had carved out an area to live here. As a jaguar shifter, she knew she shouldn't be here without permission so if she got caught she was so screwed. Wolves weren't known for being forgiving. And stealing from an alpha? She shoved those thoughts out of her head. If she was scared, she couldn't work.

Here goes nothing.

The two story house was raised like most houses on the beach but he also had an upstairs patio that she planned to use to her full advantage. She shimmied up one of the columns with a preternatural speed and hoisted herself up and over the lattice style barrier. Being a cat, she was nimble and quick on her feet, but it still took strength to do this in human form.

Crouching low to the ground, she carefully looked around the large patio at the closed French doors and then back at the beach. The waves sounded softly about a hundred yards away, the calm methodic rhythm doing little to soothe the nerves punching through her. She was about to break into an alpha's home. So, so, so stupid. But it would make her mother and sister happy.

Thankfully the quarter moon was hidden by clouds, further helping her cover. She'd been watching the Kincaid pack's comings and goings for the last week in preparation for tonight. It was midnight so almost every one of them was at one of the many bars or the hotel Kincaid owned. They all worked together as a big family. Their hours were more like vampires' than shifters', but clearly it worked for the pack because they were ridiculously wealthy.

Owning beach front property anywhere could be pricey, but they also owned an entire condominium building next door to Kincaid's personal residence. At least almost everyone was at work. And even though she knew for a fact they had a security system, she'd thrown a giant boulder through the back French doors a couple days ago in preparation.

Lauren had felt like a total jerk doing it, but she'd needed them to replace the doors. Which they'd done this morning. The chances of them having already replaced the security contact that would be standard with the system on the new doors was about five percent. More like zero percent considering she'd been watching the house practically ever since she'd ruined the doors. And when she hadn't been spying, one of her pridemates had.

As she examined the French doors now she realized the lock was also new. And it wasn't the cheap kind either. But, she was very good at getting into places she shouldn't.

Less than sixty seconds later she was inside the master bedroom. After a quick perusal of the top part of the door frame she breathed a sigh of relief to see no new contacts in place. Carefully closing the door behind her, she paused and glanced around the giant room. With her supernatural eyesight she didn't need to turn on a light to see everything—not that she would anyway. Might as well just put up a bright neon sign that she'd broken in.

The furniture was masculine, but there were definitely feminine touches. Not that Lauren cared about any of the décor. Now she was focused on looking for a safe. If he were going to hide diamonds and emeralds, it would definitely be in a safe. There was a slim chance he'd put it in a bank vault, but shifters and vamps, especially one as old as him, were weird about that stuff. No, they liked to keep their valuables close on hand.

For all she knew a silent alarm had gone off. There weren't any visible sensors in the bedroom, but that didn't mean shit. She knew that by breaking in blind without knowing the complete layout of the security system she was taking a chance but almost no one had sensors in their bedrooms. It didn't make sense. Living room areas and downstairs areas of course, but bedrooms and any upstairs saw too much foot traffic on a daily basis.

Moving quickly and quietly she went to the most obvious place to hide a safe. The closet. Nothing there. She searched behind picture frames next, then everywhere else she could think of before moving to the next room. The door was open to reveal an office.

Pausing, she could hear only the wind and waves outside. There were residual scents in the house but that made sense. She stepped inside the room, her boots silent against the rich hardwood floor. Two steps in, she realized she wasn't alone. It was like an abrupt assault on her senses and her inner animal simply knew.

Before she could turn fully around, she was tackled to the ground by a huge male. Definitely supernatural.

Strong, muscular arms encircled her from behind, throwing her to the ground, the male on top of her. Somehow he managed to angle their fall so he took the brunt of the impact on his arms. All the air left her lungs in a whoosh as panic slammed through her. She hadn't heard him, hadn't even scented him. That alone told her how dangerous he was.

Though all her animal instinct told her to fight, she knew she was at a disadvantage. Going limp, she didn't struggle. The second she was set free or her captor loosened his grip, she was running. Wolves might be strong, but jaguars were wicked fast. In human and shifter form.

"What the hell are you doing sneaking around in wolf territory in *my* alpha's fucking house?" a familiar male voice said near her ear, a trickle of his fresh scent that reminded her of the beach in winter enveloping her.

She hadn't scented him before, probably because of her own fear and panic at doing such a stupid thing—but now his scent covered her. She shivered at the sound of Max McCray's voice. Kincaid's second-in-command. He was supposed to be at the Crescent Moon Bar tonight working.

Lauren swallowed hard. "I want *my* family's fucking jewels back," she gritted out. There was no sense in lying. He'd be able to scent the bitter, acidic stench if she tried. She could normally cover her scent well, but right now she was nervous and couldn't keep her gift under control. Blind panic hummed through her, her inner jaguar telling her to run, run, *run*.

But she couldn't. Not with Max's massive body on top of her, keeping her pinned in place.

She was ashamed to admit that she'd had more than a handful of fantasies about the dark-haired, muscular shifter with the piercing blue eyes. None like this, with her flat on her stomach and him behind her... Okay, that was a lie. She'd had those types of fantasies too. Of course they'd both been naked and she hadn't been working as a thief.

COMPLETE BOOKLIST

ABOUT THE AUTHOR

Savannah Stuart is the pseudonym of *New York Times* and *USA Today* bestselling author Katie Reus. Under this name she writes slightly hotter romance than her mainstream books. Her stories still have a touch of intrigue, suspense, or the paranormal and the one thing she always includes is a happy ending. She lives in the South with her very own real life hero. In addition to writing (and reading of course!) she loves traveling with her husband.

For more information about Savannah's books please visit her website at: www.savannahstuartauthor.com.

9073475R00083

Printed in Great Britain
by Amazon.co.uk, Ltd.,
Marston Gate.